I0718365

[untitled]

issue eight

First published by Busybird Publishing 2019
Copyright © 2019 Busybird Publishing

ISBN 978-1-925949-30-8

Cover design: Kev Howlett, Busybird Publishing
Layout and typesetting: Busybird Publishing
Editing team: Alison Achter, Solonge Brave, Klurisa Hastings, Beau Hillier, Josephine Hong, Nicola Horgan, Erin McWhinney, Laura Pettenuzzo, Rhiannon Raphael, Lisa Roberts, Yee Ping Woo, Joey To, Charlotte Long, Methni Dahanayake, Cassandra Bulman, Meg Hellyer, Les Zigomanis, Blaise van Hecke.

Pinion Press
2/118 Para Road
Montmorency, Victoria
Australia 3094

Pinion Press is an imprint of Busybird Publishing
www.busybird.com.au

Contents

Editorial

Storytelling is important, and the opportunity to be able to share your story with the world is really special. Not everybody gets to do that or instigates a process to make that a reality.

Busybird's eighth edition of *[untitled]* features fifteen stories, each different in their own form, each with their own voice and character.

For some authors, it's their first publication and for others, it's something else they can add to their successes and achievements.

Short stories such as these are worth publishing because it brings together a collection of various imaginations that wouldn't otherwise be read.

Readers can expect to occupy themselves in various forms of writing, genres and styles. Each narrative is unique. Creativity is something to be celebrated and so readers can indulge in the journey of the authors and be a part of each individual narrative in the one book.

Enjoy the read!

Alison Achter.

Why I Didn't Leave the House This Week

Rhiannon Raphael

Monday

I was too overwhelmed.

As soon as I woke, my brain was buzzing with everything that urgently needed my attention. Most things had started as unimportant little errands, but then I put them off and put them off and kept putting them off until all at once I was beset by a swarm of neglected responsibilities. There were now an impossible number of decisions to be made, and I didn't have a single answer.

I tried to make a mental list as I slid my legs from under my quilt and into my waiting slippers. The longer the list grew, the more my day spiralled out of control. I felt dizzy, and stumbled into the en suite to splash cold water on my face.

So many places to visit. And every time I would have to talk to a new person. And every person would look at me. And see me. And hear whatever idiotic thing I said. And they would plaster on fake customer-service smiles to hide the fact that they were really laughing at the daft old woman in front of them. She was confused. She was possibly senile. She was such a poor old dear.

I gasped for air, struggling to suck in each tight, pained breath.

It took several hours of mixing and matching my clothes until my outfit was perfect. I couldn't leave the house looking anything other than my very best. How could I show my face in a hat that didn't match my dress? Or with a ladder in my stocking? All the neighbours would think I was losing it. They'd have a right laugh.

My hands trembled at the thought of being laughed off the street. I could barely fasten the clasps on my purse. I finally left my bedroom, and crept down the hall toward my front door. I kept my elbows tucked in so I didn't bump any of the newspaper stacks.

The front door loomed, a wooden monolith sealing the entrance to my labyrinthine home. My steps slowed, my head spun. At the last moment, I slipped sideways into my front room. I couldn't face it. The door filled me with dread; something awful must have been on the other side.

I peered through the drapes, and spotted the danger immediately. All the trees in my front garden had been vandalised. Someone – probably a group of people, probably a gang – had taken knives to the wood and carved thousands upon thousands of eyes. All staring at the house. All staring at me.

I stared back at the eyes until my vision swam and the world tilted and I collapsed. Sharp pain shot through my hips and up my back. Heart pounding, head spinning, I scrambled away until I hit a towering pillar of old paper. There I stayed, pressing my shaking hands to my face and crying helpless tears.

Tuesday

It wasn't safe outside.

The eyes burned in my head all night, making sleep impossible. Time and time again I climbed out of bed, scurried into the front room and peeked through the curtains. The eyes were always there. I couldn't count them all in the dark, so I counted the trees instead. Once I was sure that they were still where they were supposed to be, I crept back to bed, checking and re-checking the locks on the front door.

When dawn finally broke, I knew what I needed to do. I couldn't go outside and face the eyes, so I would have the trees torn down. I would find my phone book, choose a tree-removal service and then they'd be gone and my house would be safe again.

I didn't know where my phone book was, but it had to be with my papers.

There weren't just newspapers, although of course I had plenty of those. There were subscriptions to every magazine and every newspaper I could find, and I kept every copy. So many papers. And the catalogues, and the bills, letters from old friends, all those books I bought but never read, a lifetime's worth of photo albums, and another lifetime's worth of diaries and journals …

I usually stored all the papers in great tottering stacks pushed up against the walls, but lately I'd noticed the spaces between the stacks getting narrower. It was harder to move back and forth between the rooms in my house without getting lost. The stacks fell more often, and I was trapped for hours at a time.

I wandered the twisted corridors of my house from top to bottom. It took hours because every fifteen minutes I had to hurry back downstairs to count the trees and check the locks. I didn't find the phone book against any of the walls.

There was no choice then. It was time for a proper clean.

Wednesday

I had too much to do.

I filled the bathtub in the upstairs bathroom with as much paper as it would hold. Then I dropped a lit match inside and burned it all.

The paper was old and brittle. It caught quickly, and flared bright and hot. While the first lot of papers were reduced to ash, I kept adding more and more. When the soot and cinders piled too high, I turned on the taps and washed it down the drain. Then I'd refill the tub, and start the burning over again.

I emptied half of the upstairs hall like this before the smoke started making me dizzy.

I wanted to keep all of the windows closed and bolted, with the curtains drawn tight. I knew that was the only way to be safe. But the smoke was too thick, the fire too hot. It made my eyes water, and the skin of my face and throat itch. I coughed until my hands were black. And there was still so much left to burn.

I finally gave in, and opened the skylight in the bathroom. It worked a treat. All the smoke got pulled up and out, and I could keep burning.

The more I burned, the more quickly I moved. The heat from the flames seeped into me, melted away weakness and frailty, and replaced them with enough energy to keep my body moving in time with my racing thoughts. I felt ten years younger as I pulled down another stack of old newspapers, humming to myself as I dragged them upstairs and into the bathroom.

But the skylight troubled me. Opening it was like taking the bandage off a fresh wound, exposing my insides to the elements. It was more dangerous than painting an open target on the roof of my house and daring something to try and get inside.

Thursday

Something got inside.

It came in through the skylight – that damned skylight! I was in the bathroom doing more burning. The thing swooped in like a shadow and disappeared into the smoke before I could get a good look at it. All I heard was the sharp snap of feathers slicing air.

I screamed and wrenched the taps. Water poured into the bathtub, immediately dousing the flames. Great plumes of smoke and steam rose and filled the air. I couldn't see the creature. I couldn't breathe. It was here. Inside my house. It had come for me.

I froze in place, too terrified to move. The bottom of the tub was clogged with sodden black paper, and its sides streaked with damp black ash. I couldn't hear the thing anymore. Where was it hiding? The fumes swirled around me, too thick and too grey and too close. I felt surrounded. Was there really only one? Or were there many hidden in the smoke, creeping toward me from every angle?

Then, I heard it. A low rasp, like scales scraping over metal. And a soft hiss.

It was at the tap!

I lunged, but was too slow. By the time my fumbling fingers had closed around the tap, the thing had already vanished into the pipe.

I could hear the hissing again, echoing down towards me, and this time it sounded like laughter.

Friday

I was being followed.

The hissing was with me everywhere I went. The thing used the pipes to slither through the house. I spent the day tearing old towels into strips and shoving them into faucets and down drains. If I could cut it off – trap it inside the pipes behind the walls – then at least it wouldn't be able to get to me.

Because I was certain that was what it wanted. That's why it followed me so closely, hissing in a voice like rotten fruit — too sticky to be sweet. It was waiting for its chance to strike out at me from an unblocked drain. But I wouldn't give it a chance.

It was early afternoon by the time I was done. I stood in the downstairs toilet, panting and wiping sweat off my face, having just finished clogging the bowl with an old beach towel. Finally, I was safe.

Then the phone rang. I hobbled back out into the hall to answer it. When I picked up the receiver, all I could hear was familiar hissing laughter.

'You didn't really think I was in the walls, did you?' the thing said. Its voice was changing as it spoke, becoming less like a hiss and more like a growl.

I stayed silent. My mouth was filled with bile that tasted like rotten fruit and my skin itched all over, a thousand fingernails racing across my skin.

'I'm not in the walls. I'm in the *house*,' the voice growled, near giddy with triumph.

'There's nowhere you can go where you'll be free of me.'

Saturday

I couldn't get out of bed.

I saw no reason to get up, let alone try to leave. What would be the point?

The thing had freed itself from the pipes at some point during the night. It had taken a physical form again, and I could see it clearly now. It wasn't a bird, as I had originally thought, or a serpent, like I had come to suspect. It was a dog; a huge dog with fur so black it was like staring into a void.

It nosed its way through my bedroom door, padded across the room towards me, and climbed up onto the mattress. It settled beside me, with its head resting on my leg, and started to grow.

I had lost interest in trying to burn my collection of papers. I had difficulty remembering why I had even started in the first place. I knew that the reason had seemed terribly important at the time, but the urgency was dull now. It felt like I was experiencing everything through a thick haze of indifference, and beside me the dog grew to the size of a horse.

Even though it was difficult to feel anything at the moment, the guilt somehow still found its way through. I had started this week with such a long list of tasks, and now I couldn't even be bothered to get out of bed. And there was no one to blame but myself. I was such a waste of space.

The black dog was now so large that it filled my entire bedroom.

I had a vague sense that I should be doing something about my current state, something to fix the way I was feeling, or at least the way I was acting. But I was so tired. More tired than I had ever been in my life. If I could just get some rest, then I would be able to handle things again.

I napped for a few hours, but woke up feeling even more exhausted than before.

The black dog was impossibly huge, filling the room, spilling out into the halls and down the stairs. I could feel its entire weight on the bed. Its huge head still resting on my leg, pinning me to the mattress. It was all my fault. I was pathetic, too lazy to get out of bed, to go outside and run a few simple errands. What was wrong with me? Why was I always so full of excuses not to leave the house?

Sunday
It was raining.

Threads

Fran Collings

We touch down in Bangkok to a steamy, early morning. I breathe in a humid mix of exhaust fumes, spices and flowers as we check into our hotel. We need to rest, in preparation for the journey ahead.

'We go visit village together, Kannika,' Aunt had said. 'You fifteen now. Time see how lucky I bring you to Australia. Time meet Grandmother Yai. She care for you from tiny baby.'

The night bus for Khon Kaen departs at 9:30 and we clamber aboard, our cases crammed with gifts for the village. The trip is dark and chilly, with the air-con ramped up to just below freezing. I squirm against the vinyl seat and sleep fitfully. Maybe Grandmother

Yai can help me. I long to know more of my birth-mother – as well as my true birthdate, instead of one hatched from handwritten village records. I stumble from the bus in the early morning, numb, disoriented.

Aunt Sukanya is already ahead, waving to a slight man with a thatch of dark hair.

'Kannika, this is Uncle Nakul, my oldest brother.'

'*Sa-wat-dee kâ,*' I say, remembering to *wâi*, my hands pointed in prayer.

Uncle Nakul has dark, coffee bean eyes, which shine as he helps heave our luggage onto the tray of his utility. As soon as we climb into the cabin, he accelerates abruptly, with a crunch of gears and squeal of tyres.

Once we leave Khon Kaen, we drive for an hour past emerald-green rice paddies. People are working on the terraces and I see water buffalo, black, broad-backed beasts with conical horns. We pass sparse dwellings on stilts, scrambled together from wood, corrugated iron and palm-fronds. Most have drooping balconies. I try to recall the village of my childhood, but can picture only the photos Aunt has shown me from her last visit.

Suddenly, Uncle veers right. The vehicle bounces along a deeply rutted track and pulls into a village cramped with stilted, sagging houses. Chickens flap, stirring up dust, as Uncle Nakul leaps down and swings open the passenger door.

Villagers emerge from their homes as we arrive. Aunt pushes me forward to greet them. One girl, her hair in shiny black braids, steps forward shyly. She offers a bunch of fresh flowers, then presses her tiny hands together in a graceful *wâi*.

'Welcome,' she says in schoolgirl English. 'My name is Noon and I am so happy to meet you.'

I scarcely have time to return her greeting before she rushes forward to hug me, thick plaits bouncing on butterfly-thin shoulders. I breathe in her scent of coconut oil and flowers.

'*Sa-wat-dee kâ*,' an old woman's voice silences the chattering crowd.

'It is Grandmother Yai,' whispers Sukanya.

'*Sa-wat-dee kâ*,' I say, making a deep *wâi*.

Grandmother is almost square, as wide as she is tall, and wears a long brown dress, patterned with golden flowers. Her hair is nearly white but her eyes are button bright, and she bears a dark mole on her cheek. Her voice and smile sit just on the edge of my memory. I run to hug her.

'*Korpkun kâ*, Yai (thank you, Grandmother),' I say.

'*Jong ya-reun* (bless you),' she replies.

The villagers amble away as Yai leads us to her home. On the way, she indicates the palm-thatched long house where we will sleep tonight. Yai's home is simply decorated, with a small brass statue of the Buddha, and a pair of richly embroidered wall hangings of elephants. We sit on dark blue and gold triangular cushions with backrests, as Yai brings us small bowls of *johnk* (rice gruel) and a plate of hard-boiled eggs. I dutifully eat a little of the *johnk*, but can only manage one of the eggs. Next, Yai offers a tray of fragrant, golden mangos and cups of unsweetened black tea.

Gentle conversation laps between Yai and Sukanya. I try to follow but become lost in the maze of words, which sound like a long-lost lullaby. I drift off to sleep, and wake to a sharp elbow in my ribs.

'Kannika, that is very rude!' Sukanya hisses.

'What? Sorry. I didn't mean to sleep, Aunt.' I immediately sit up on the cushions.

'No, I mean your feet. They are pointing towards Yai! Tuck them beneath you.'

Now I understand. To point your feet towards anyone is considered disrespectful. Hastily I curl them back, just as Uncle Nakul appears, ready to escort us to the long house.

Aunt and I climb rickety steps and find two sleeping mats already rolled in one corner. Long leaf shadows weave through gaps in the wooden walls, creating an airy tree house. A small stool stands in a far corner. It holds an enamel basin and two neatly folded thin towels, with a tall jug of water alongside.

'We rest now, Kannika,' says Aunt. 'Tonight will be welcome feast.'

By mid-afternoon, there is chatter and laughter as the village children return from school. Noon calls from below; she wants to show me the village. I smell the pigs before I see them. They are mottled black-pink, with long snouts snuffling within the wooden slats of their sty. The smell is intense: manure, over-ripe fruit and stinking mud. They squeal shrilly as Noon tosses them scraps, before we visit the chickens. Some hens are beady-eyed, with shiny black feathers shimmering iridescent green; others are motherly, brown-speckled matrons, with lush red combs and stumpy legs.

'These hens are ours,' says Noon, pointing to some of the matrons, squatting comfortably on straw-filled car-tyre nests.

The village cooking fires are being stoked, shooting golden firefly sparks against the darkening sky. A neon light fastened to a slanting pole flutters to life.

'You have electricity!'

'Sometimes.' Noon smiles. She points to a second power pole, close by the village entrance. It is festooned with coils of cable, black leads draping across the village to various dwellings.

'So, everyone just taps off?' I ask.

Noon laughs. 'If there are too many at once, it is finished.'

Together we walk back to the long house and Noon helps carry our gifts to the communal eating area. Aunt stands beside me as we offer them. Our first gift is for Yai. She strokes the rainbow colours of patchwork quarters with matching threads and smiles.

'Now Uncle Nakul,' nudges Sukanya. We give Uncle a wristwatch with an impressive number of lights and buttons. He grins broadly. When I hand him reels of fishing line and hooks, his smile deepens. I think his face will disappear into the wrinkles, leaving only his gap-toothed smile.

Aunt and I give gifts to the others, and for Noon there is a gold pendant, with a sapphire set in its flower-like centre. The stone sends tiny flecks of light around the fire as she fastens it on her neck.

One woman does not step forward to receive her gifts. She remains apart from the group, standing in the shadows. I cannot make out her face, but can see her eyes, fixed on me, shining in the darkness.

'Who is she?' I whisper to Aunt.

'That is Natcha,' she replies, as if that explains everything.

Aunt takes my arm and draws me towards the feast. Mats have been spread on the ground for seating. There are some plastic chairs, but not enough for all. Natcha steps forward to claim one and I see her clearly now; her lank hair straggling, unkempt, over a long, sullen face. Perhaps sensing my gaze, Natcha turns to me. She scowls, mouth down-turned, twisted into a snarl. Her black eyes gleam, spider-like, trapping me within their glare.

The feast is generous, with platters of crisp and succulent roast pork, jasmine rice, long strands of wheat and egg noodles, dishes of *larb-gai* (chicken salad), and *sôm-dam*, the green papaya salad that Sukanya often makes at home.

Yai has prepared sticky rice for sweets. She scoops it from bamboo cooking baskets, and serves it with sweet, golden mangoes. She spoons thick coconut cream over the top. Afterwards, we gather and talk well into the night.

Later in the long house, as I rest on my sleeping mat, I want to ask about Natcha, but Sukanya is already snoring. I manage to fall asleep, but wake to the sound of heavy shuffling and snuffling around the long house. Something bumps a pole, sending tremors along the floor.

I touch Aunt's arm. 'What is that?' I ask.

'Water buffalo,' she mumbles. 'They sometimes roam through the village after dark.' She rolls over, turning her back to me. I remain awake, sweating on my thin sleeping mat and longing for my bed back home. The village feels strange, alien; I can scarcely believe that I was born here. Aunt already seems a different person, with ways I do not recognise. My mind prickles with restless thoughts: the smells, the roaming buffalo and, most of all, Natcha.

Long before the sun slips through the slats, the village roosters are astir.

Tendrils of smoke curl from the fire; people are boiling water, making rice porridge and sharing leftovers from last night's feast. Aunt and I rise and splash tepid water on our faces. We dress and clamber down the steps. Yai greets us, and says that later we can shower in her small bathroom. We breakfast together and Noon joins us, anxious to show me the rice paddies. Yai has other plans.

'Tomorrow *Phuk Siaw* festival begin,' Aunt says. 'Today Yai says we buy silk to make *fai pooh kaan* (sacred threads). We have monk bless them. Tie them on wrists of friends, relations. It sign of love, good feeling,' Aunt explains. 'Uncle Nakul will drive us, Noon come too.'

After breakfast and a shower, we pile into Uncle's utility. Sukanya sits beside Yai in the front seat. I climb into the back with Noon and several other villagers. Natcha squeezes in at the last minute, forcing us all to move up uncomfortably. She glowers at me over each bump of the fifty kilometre journey. I smile, offer a tremulous '*sa-wat-dee kâ*', but her black eyes do not flicker. In the silk village we choose threads, under Yai's guidance. The silks come in soft, glowing gold, pink, crimson, green and blue; nature's colours.

After returning to our village, I walk to the rice paddies with Noon and her friends.

'Can you tell me more about Natcha?' I ask as we stroll along the road.

'Natcha is … just Natcha.' Noon shrugs. 'She had a little girl, long time ago. But something happened – that's all I know.'

I decide to ask Sukanya when I return. I wonder why she seems reluctant to speak of Natcha. Once back, Sukanya draws me aside.

'Tonight we make meal for village. I cook chicken and *larb-gai*. You, Kannika, boil jasmine rice. Later Yai help you make sticky rice and fruit. Show village you can cook Thai way.'

Late afternoon, I wash rice and pour it into the large cooking pot to boil. Natcha sits in one of the plastic chairs, placed so as to have a good view of my preparations. Next, I roll out the long dining mats. I have just set them out as a black piglet escapes. Boys chase it through the village, whooping, spurting dust over my carefully spread mats. Now I must shake them and begin again. As I lift them, an acrid smell drifts from the rice pot. It has boiled dry, leaving behind a sticky mess to scour. There is a sudden harsh caw, like the call of a malevolent crow.

It is Natcha, cackling, mouth wide open, revealing blackened stumps of teeth.

I soon discover that I am in disgrace, now known throughout the village as 'the one who cannot boil rice'. Sukanya and Yai seem deeply ashamed. Natcha, on the other hand, appears jubilant. Noon sits beside me and squeezes my hand. During dinner, everyone in the village laughs at me, and Natcha laughs the most of all.

Later, people sit, talking – but after my shame I feel like an intruder. I leave quietly for the long house and curl up on my sleeping mat. I fall asleep, and do not hear the water buffalo that night.

I awake to see Aunt already dressed, her long hair freshly braided.

'Aunt,' I ask, 'Natcha seemed happy that I spoiled the rice. Why does she dislike me so much?'

'Not now, Kannika. It nearly time for breakfast. If you hurry, I braid your hair.'

I bathe from the wash bowl, put on a fresh shirt and sarong, and stand, my dark hair cascading down my back. 'I'm leaving my hair loose today,' I say.

I know I must find my place in the village, understand where I would have fitted in if I had stayed. There must be a reason why Natcha is already my enemy. If Aunt will not answer my questions, then I shall ask Grandmother Yai. I follow Aunt to breakfast. I spoon rice into a bowl, slice some papaya and sit alone in the sunlight.

After breakfast, Yai shows us her quilt workshop. Inside, many silken and cotton quilts hang from the walls. This simple room is made rich through Yai's skilled stitching, and some help from the ancient Singer treadle crammed into a corner. I take Yai's hands in mine and tell her how clever she is. She smiles, explaining that she sews and sells the quilts so that she can keep the village children in her care.

'You one of those children, Kannika. Grandmother Yai care for you, before I bring you to Australia,' Aunt reminds me.

My eyes ache with tears. I am tired of always feeling grateful to Aunt. I cannot spend the rest of my life this way. Grandmother Yai frowns. She nods at me to go ahead. As I walk back to the long house, I see her take Aunt aside.

Later, Yai invites us both back to her small home, and makes tea. As we sit on the floor cushions, I am careful to tuck my feet beneath me. Yai tells me she is ready to answer my questions. I lift my cup with both hands, inhaling the jasmine scent as I wonder what to ask first.

'My mother, what did she look like?' I say.

Yai shuffles over to a carved chest and extracts a photograph. It is grainy, black and white. In the photo a young woman stands beside a statue. She is slim, with dark hair scooped upwards, her eyes wide open as if surprised. She wears a modest long-sleeved top and a dark sarong. Yai places the photo into my hands. She smiles. It is mine to keep.

'Has my mother ever returned to the village?' I ask. 'Do you know where she is now?'

Grandmother touches my hand. 'After your mother leave village, no word. She never come back. So sorry.'

'My father then, where is he?'

'Him I not know. He not of this village.'

My heart beats fast as I ask my third question. I hope it will prove that I am a real person, and not some orphan girl with a birthdate plucked from the sky. 'Yai, when was I born? Do you know the real date?' I whisper.

'I only know it lychee season.' Yai bows her head.

Lychee season lasts from April to June. I slump against my cushion. This is the closest I will ever come to discovering my birthdate. Yai closes her eyes, but I have one last question. 'Yai, who is Natcha, and why does she dislike me so?'

'Natcha unhappy woman.' Yai opens her eyes, peers into my face. 'At time Sukanya took you Australia, I look after Natcha's child too. Her name Arisa, your little friend.' Yai smiles. 'You run in village, hold hand together. When you have chance leave with Sukanya, Natcha want it be Arisa. *"Take Arisa with you,"* she cry.'

'But I must choose you,' shrugs Aunt, as she takes up the story. 'You my best friend's daughter, after all. She still my friend, in my heart. When I return village, from working Bangkok, you already small girl. I cannot leave you behind.'

Yai's plump face looks suddenly drawn and old.

'Come, Kannika,' chides Aunt. 'So many questions bring sadness. You make Grandmother Yai too tired. We leave her rest now.'

As we return to the long house, I press Aunt to tell me more about Natcha.

'You come Australia with me, Arisa stay in village with Natcha. That is all story.' Aunt turns from me abruptly. 'Now we rest before Uncle Nakul drive us Khon Kaen this afternoon.'

Once Aunt is asleep, breathing steadily, I move softly to the steps and walk to Grandmother Yai's house. The whole village is silent. Maybe everyone is resting before the festival tonight. Perhaps Grandmother Yai is also sleeping. Hesitantly, I tap on her door.

She opens it instantly. She seems to have been expecting me.

'Grandmother Yai.' I make a deep *wâi.* 'So sorry to disturb you.'

'Come, Kannika. You need ask more?'

I nod. She points to the blue cushions and I sit. Grandmother Yai squats beside me.

'I must know more about Natcha,' I blurt. 'Aunt will not tell me.'

Yai has just made a fresh cup of tea and offers one to me. I shake my head. Yai cradles her own cup and leans forward; her dark eyes stare into mine.

'When you go, Natcha in very black mood, long time. Always bad temper, that one. When she look after Arisa, she too sad watch that little one. Arisa run, one day, to rice paddies. When Natcha miss Arisa, it too late. Channels full of water. Very deep. They find little Arisa face down, in reeds. Then Natcha angry and so sad. She bitter. She think Arisa run away, to look for her friend. She think you, Kannika, took Arisa's hope of good life.'

I feel numb, shocked. Such a sad story, and one in which I had, unknowingly, played a part. My cheeks are wet and I am sorry for Natcha too. Now I understand, a little.

Grandmother Yai pats my knee. 'Remember always, child,' she says gently, 'it no one's fault.'

Later in the afternoon, Uncle Nakul drives us into Khon Kaen. Yai will take the silk threads to the temple, for blessing, while we are gone. Noon, and our friends and cousins, climb into the back of the utility. Natcha comes too. Now I see the sadness beneath her scowls, and greet her, but still she does not speak.

Uncle Nakul guides us to the market to select food for tonight's farewell dinner. It is to celebrate the *Phuk Siaw* festival, as well as our last night in the village.

On our return, I sit with Noon and her friends, helping sort the sacred threads.

When the meal ends, everyone helps clear away dishes and food, ready for the festival. Aunt and I give *fai pook kaan* to our friends and relatives and I clasp several woven bands in my hands.

Friends have already tied cords around my wrist – gold, crimson, pink and blue. I give one to Natcha, and she takes my golden cord, but offers nothing in return. As I exchange bands with Yai, Aunt, Uncle Nakul and Noon, I realise these sacred threads are bonding friends into family, creating lifelong ties with friends and relatives alike. I begin to feel a small sense of belonging.

Late at night, the village falls dark and quiet as I lie awake in the long house, re-living the last three days. My early life is no longer a distant dream. It is here, now, with real sights, smells, sounds, and people who have known me since birth. As I rest on my sleeping mat, I hear the soft thud of buffalo hooves, listen to their moist snuffles as they nose around the long house poles. I am no longer afraid – perhaps I shall even miss them a little.

The first rooster crows well before dawn. I rise and creep down the steps. I stand on the damp earth, absorbing the half-remembered sounds and scents of my childhood. The morning mist smells of buffalo dung, chickens, pigs and the spicy remains of last night's feast.

A light glows in Yai's house, across the village. She is already preparing breakfast, before Uncle Nakul drives us into Khon Kaen for our flight home. As I stand in the misty half-light, a figure steps silently beside me. I gasp, then I see it is Natcha. Her lips are skewed into a smile, and she makes a small, barely perceptible *wâi*. Her bony fingers clasp my wrist. I almost cry out, then realise she wishes only to bind it with a sacred thread. I feel her breath, warm, sweet-sour, as she leans close.

'You born May, night of new moon,' she whispers, 'same my Arisa.'

She *wâis* again and slides softly away.

Types of Oranges I've Never Eaten

Ashley Kalagian Blunt

The type of orange your mother lovingly places in a red and green stocking, with your name embroidered in gold thread and hung in front of a crackling wood fireplace on Christmas Eve.

The type of orange swiped off your little brother's placemat while your mother's back is to you, rubber gloves to her elbows and hands submerged in greasy dishwater.

The type of orange your grandfather grows in his orchard, which belonged to his father and was planted by his father before him. As you sample the new season crop, your fingernails digging into the fruit's tough but yielding rind, he puts his hand on your shoulder and casts his eyes beyond the groves to where the sun sets into the Pacific calm. One day, he says, this will all belong to you and your brother.

The type of orange that is piled with two hundred others in a wooden street-vendor cart on a cobblestone corner in the slanting sunshine of a crisp January afternoon. The sun-wizened Turkish man squeezes several of the oranges in the medieval-looking machine at the head of the cart, and you pay him a few lira for a plastic cup filled with juice so sweet the nerves of your teeth scream, and then, minutes later, drop the cup in a pile of garbage because there is no street-side recycling in Istanbul.

The type of orange your new love plucks from a wicker picnic basket and peels, a fine spray bursting, so he can brush your lips slowly with one perfect segment, its ripe scent and cool touch flooding your senses as you lie under a canopy of flowering jacarandas.

The type of orange that is the synthetic flavouring of the caffeine tablets you're relying on, and even synthetic, the smell evokes the orchard. How exactly did your great-great-grandfather come to own the land outside Bundaberg? It hardly matters, since your brother suggested selling the orchard-operation rights to that multinational and focusing instead on holding company acquisitions, which has been keeping you at the office all hours, and a more pressing question is how you're going to reconcile these earning projection statements, and even more pressing, where are the rest of your caffeine pills?

Blood oranges.

The type of orange that is a just-because-it's-Tuesday surprise from *him*, a gift-wrapped navel orange made of orange-flavoured dark chocolate, though frankly it's probably all chemical flavouring and there's not a single atom of actual orange involved. But still, when you unwrap it, the dimpled slices break apart, and the flavour is rich and nuanced and complex and so is your love.

The Hamlin orange your housemate chucks at you when you've been studying nine hours straight, which hits you in the spine like a punch and you both laugh, because it's definitely time to put on your miniskirt with the electric blue sequins and those knee-high boots that always give you blisters but are totally worth it, and right before leaving you check your bank account to discover that your mom still hasn't put through that transfer and you fire off a text full of red frowny faces.

The type of bitter, inedible orange pulled from a branch overhanging the fence of a ramshackle house outside Colonia, Uruguay, where you and your no-longer-new love have hired a moped but no helmets, and the sun warms your back while the wind splits the skin of your knuckles open, and you drop the orange to the ground, wondering what you will have for dinner in Buenos Aires that evening.

The type of orange that becomes marmalade with ginger and lime in your sister-in-law's kitchen. Each jar with a decorative square of fabric over the lid, wrapped in a green ribbon. Six of them in a box with a birthday card that includes her new recipe. The box delivered along with a bouquet of white carnations as a surprise birthday breakfast. You don't like white carnations.

The type of orange that is sliced, oven-dried, and dropped into a negroni, a perfectly bitter cocktail for sipping while your business partners talk over you.

Those cherry-sized oranges they grow in Japan. Maybe you can get a crate shipped. Where's your EA?

The type of orange that is artisanally preserved and sliced onto a white cake flavoured with orange oil and served at the end of a four-course meal in the type of restaurant where the tablecloths are white linen and there are two types of wine glasses on every table. You spend most of the salad course telling your husband about a dream you had, the one where you worked in a car manufacturing company where the entire factory was robots, but that was the thing because you were a robot too, and isn't that so symbolic? Except when you break off in the middle of a sentence, he doesn't notice and a minute later says for the second time that his steak is a little overdone, and you order the orange cake to share because you really only want a bite, and now the slice is in front of you, and you lift a forkful of fluffy, moist cake into your mouth and taste the essence of vanilla mingled with orange, one delicate crumb clinging to your lip.

The type where it turns out all men are men and women can't help but sacrifice themselves on their patriarchal altar because they've been raised in a culture that demands nothing less, and also there's an orange involved.

An orange that has been passed from hand to hand, to truck, to ship, back to hand, to rest finally in your manicured grasp, its skin gleaming like an advertisement, as though it had always been meant to come to you, as though you had been chosen – picked – instead of lucky.

One of the 97 per cent of oranges belonging to the world's most fortunate two per cent, the two per cent you'd never consider yourself part of, because it's not like you chose to be born to the son of an orchard owner who happened to have a head for business, a knack for the international export game, who taught you that scruples are a sign of weakness, and to take what you can get when the getting is good.

The type of orange where your husband of so many years, shrewd and focused, introduces you to the right people and talks up your successes and has never complained that your annual bonus surpasses his, though honestly you wish he'd just pack a picnic, or forget the picnic, and just take you to bed and squeeze a ripe, dripping orange over your chest, or maybe line your navel with sliced strawberries.

The type of orange that rhymes.

The type of fit-in-your-palm orange that comes individually wrapped in lime-green tissue paper in a box of identically wrapped oranges, and when you pull back the tissue, you find a soft patch of greenish-white fuzz advancing across the mushy flesh.

The type of orange that comes in an oversized corporate fruit basket delivered to your thirtieth-storey office with a view of the harbour, nestled in shredded, mauve-tinted crepe paper among apples, bananas and a single pineapple, along with various caramel and chocolate dips, and two bottles of sparkling wine, all in recognition of the deal you closed that afternoon. You smile even though you know the deal wasn't a hundred per cent above board, and in fact may have broken a couple of obscure laws and crossed some hazy ethical lines, and will cost you your career if you're ever found out. The fruit is flavourless, picked too early, but the wine is crisp.

The type of orange that is the exact syrupy flavour of the neon-coloured throat lozenges you have been sucking for weeks before you finally go to the doctor the day after your thirty-eighth birthday for a series of increasingly unpleasant appointments and procedures, until you realise you should have said yes when your sister-in-law offered to accompany you today, because now you are in the stairwell, an Everest of wadded tissues in your lap, wondering why the doctor felt the need to draw the squamous cells, the thin, flat cells that line the inside of the larynx, her eyes fixed on the prescription pad where her pen outlined lumpy circles in the tube of a disembodied throat.

The type of orange where, after slicing cleanly through the rind and biting into each glistening segment, juice dripping off your chin, you can say *that was satisfying* with the conviction that at its centre this world is decent and good.

Kitchen Anatomy

Pamela Baker

Rose reads the glossy magazines in the doctor's waiting room: *House and Garden*, *Better Homes*, even *Vogue Living*. She eases her stiff hips onto a chair and flips to the kitchen feature, as she always does. She knows exactly what the latest fashion in kitchens is, although she's not sure if she likes those stainless steel fridges and stoves. They remind her of hospitals. She had enough of hospitals with Donnie after his father was killed. There's nothing homely about stainless steel.

The *Vogue Living* kitchen is cold and white except for the silvery fridge and stove, and the flecks of grey in the marble benches. Even the floor is made of chilly white tile.

Rose shifts on the hard chair, turning the pages, studying each picture carefully. None of the magazines ever mention prices. How much *would* a new kitchen cost?

She'd been overwhelmed when the letter came from a solicitor with the news that her brother George had left her some shares. Dear George. She hadn't known he owned any shares, let alone that he'd leave them to her. The nice man at the solicitor's has sold the shares for her. This morning she put twenty thousand dollars in her bank account. She has never had so much money in her whole life.

House and Garden falls open at a kitchen that is warm golden wood. *Classic design* the caption says. She gazes at the wooden cupboards, the polished wood floor, and the round wooden table and chairs. She imagines having breakfast with Donnie at that table. It would be like living in a forest.

The surgery door opens. Rose closes *House and Garden,* stacking the magazines neatly back on the table. She hobbles into the surgery.

'Now, Rose,' the doctor says, 'you have to look after yourself. Those ulcers are playing up, aren't they?'

Rose nods.

The doctor wraps the blood pressure sleeve around her arm. He puts the stethoscope in his ears and begins to pump.

'Mmm,' he says. 'I'll give you another prescription, but you must slow down.' He checks the screen on his computer. 'You're seventy-five now. You're not still doing that cleaning work for the council, are you?'

Rose shakes her head.

'I could get *you* some home help.'

'I'm not an old lady, Doctor.'

The doctor smiles. 'How's Donnie?'

Rose makes a quick up-and-down movement of her shoulders. 'He's doing a TAFE course now. He'll have his VCE by the end of next year.'

She beams at the doctor. Perhaps … but she knows Donnie will never work. He's too highly strung; he needs a steady routine and no stress at all. He went to pieces when Tom was killed. Poor lamb saw his father walk under the truck and never got over it. When she had the flu last year Donnie was wild-eyed by the time she could get out of bed without feeling giddy. He burnt two saucepans and spilled hot fat all over the floor. It went under the fridge and splashed up the wall. She had to get Jean's husband from next door to help her move the fridge so she could scrub underneath. His face went so red she worried he'd have a heart attack; she was about to run next door to get their son. 'We'll soon have a doctor in the house,' Jean says, at least once a week.

'If we had a proper kitchen,' Donnie said, his lips thin and pursed, 'this sort of accident wouldn't happen.'

They bought the house cheap in one of those brief periods when Tom stopped drinking and had a proper job. He pulled down the lean-to kitchen but was back on the grog before he got around to building a new one. She's made do with the old laundry on the back verandah for more years than she likes to count.

'How old is Donnie now?' the doctor asks.

Rose has to stop and think. Her eldest grandchild turned twenty-three last year. She counts on her fingers. 'That makes Wendy … the miscarriages … so Donnie must be … forty-three, Doctor,' she says.

The doctor sighs. 'Tell him to come in for a check up. I haven't seen him for a while. Need to keep an eye on his medication.'

'He's doing very well at TAFE, Doctor,' she says.

'Maybe he'll be able to start looking after you soon.'

Before she leaves the surgery, Rose finds the page with the wooden kitchen in *House and Garden*. She leaves it open on the table.

The lady from the kitchen store wears a black suit and high-heeled shoes. Her long silver earrings tinkle when she moves her head. Rose can't imagine her cooking. Her eyes widen when Rose shows her out the back.

'Hang on a tick while I turn the gas down,' Rose says. The big stock pot is bubbling on the stove. The lady from the store makes a shivery movement with her shoulders. Rose beams at her. 'I keep the back door open while I'm cooking. There's no ventilation.' The big lad who came with the lady doesn't meet Rose's eye. She wonders if he's the one who'll build the kitchen. He wears jeans and an open-necked shirt, carries a notebook and one of those steel measuring tapes in a little case. He fills the doorway while the lady walks around, her heels clicking on the concrete floor where the old troughs used to be.

'I can see why you want a new kitchen,' the lady says. Rose has forgotten her name. 'The *Country Life Style*, wasn't it?' In the book of designs at the store Rose found *the* kitchen, just like the one she'd seen in the magazine. The lady shivers again. 'Must be a bit chilly in the winter.'

'We just wear our woollies,' Rose says. The smell from the stock pot is good. Donnie's favourite pea soup. When the lady leaves Rose will scrape the bacon from the bones and suck the last bit off before putting the bones in the rubbish bin. If Donnie's home early, she'll let him suck the bones.

'The lad'll measure up now and we'll send you a quote.' The lady looks doubtful. She whispers something in the lad's ear.

'Would you like a bowl of soup before you leave?' Rose asks. The lady smiles and shakes her head. To measure up the boy has to move the table and chairs and the old dresser that Rose bought at the op shop. He puts his arms around the fridge and lifts it away from the wall as if it were made of cardboard.

'Your fridge has seen better days,' the lady says.

When the quote comes in the post Rose has to sit down. Twenty-five thousand dollars. It must be a mistake.

Another kitchen place in the next suburb quotes thirty thousand dollars. It's not as though she wants gold-plated taps and marble benches. She'd thought the money from the shares was a fortune. She won't give up. Donnie will have a proper kitchen when she's gone.

'You don't live forever,' she says to Jean, who makes sympathetic noises about the cost of the new kitchen.

'What about a small bank loan?' Jean suggests as she arranges Arum lilies from the garden in a crystal vase.

Rose reminds herself of the lady from the kitchen store when she dresses in her best navy suit to visit the bank where she has had an account all of her life. She carries her passbook in her handbag.

'Nobody has those passbooks anymore, Mum,' Wendy told her. 'Get a card and then you can withdraw your money free of charge from the ATM.'

Rose doesn't like machines.

'They don't charge me to withdraw my money,' she tells her daughter. 'People over fifty-five get free banking.' It seems wrong to her. Banks used to pay *you* interest for lending them your money. It's not as though it takes much looking after. They just put it in that big vault and forget about it.

'It's the account management,' Wendy explains. Rose shakes her head.

Rose waits nervously while the bank manager works out the interest she will need to pay to borrow the extra money. The amount is shocking.

'It's your age,' the bank manager explains. 'We'll need the deed to the house, of course. As collateral.'

On her way home, she notices a sticker on the back of a car: *Don't take your organs to heaven. Heavens knows we need them here.* One of her granddaughters is an organ donor. If she dies in an accident, like Tom, her granddaughter's heart or her lungs or any other bits and pieces can be given to some poor soul who needs them. Even the corneas from her eyes.

'You're too old to be an organ donor, Gran,' her granddaughter said, and screwed up her nose. 'Imagine your liver, all wrinkly, like crepe paper.' They'd laughed until they cried. Rose has read about people in some of those poor countries selling a kidney to wealthy Americans. And the chauffeur to that Packer man gave his boss one of his kidneys. She'd give Donnie or Wendy or any of the grandchildren one of hers. Except that her kidneys are too old. She'd even sell a kidney to get the new kitchen. One kidney will see her out. Rose sighs.

She phones another bank. 'Do I have to come down and get the forms?' she asks. 'I'm nearly eighty.' Poor sad old lady, she can hear the young woman on the phone thinking.

'No, we'll send them, my dear. You look after yourself.'

Rose suppresses a giggle. The information with the forms will explain about the interest, the girl at the bank tells her. She sounds as if she's about fifteen.

But the other bank is nearly as greedy. It makes no sense to her to borrow five thousand dollars if she has to pay back so much more than she originally needed. If only she could return to the council job and earn the money. As soon as they found out she was seventy they asked her to leave.

Rose gives the old dresser a shake. The plates and cups rattle. She stares at the painted wooden ceiling. The rain used to come in where the verandah roof meets the roof of the house. She had that repaired after Tom was killed. With three dollars in the bank, she asked for an overdraft and paid it back with one of her illegal jobs: cleaning her supervisor's house. Her supervisor left the cash on the table, under the sugar bowl. Nobody wants to employ her anymore. She can't save five thousand dollars from the pension. It took her fifteen years to save the five thousand dollars she's put away to pay for her funeral, so that Donnie, and Wendy – who's always struggling to manage with her four – won't have to worry when she dies.

'I don't know how I'm going to get the extra money,' Rose says to Jean. Jean's kitchen has lots of cupboards, a proper sink, and laminex benches. Instead of benches Rose has a large chopping board propped over the laundry trough.

Jean pours Rose a cup of tea. 'Michael's on to real bodies this week,' she says. 'Not just pictures in textbooks.' Her eyes are wide and she's smiling, lips pressed together, eyebrows raised. 'Michael's named his body Carmel.' She makes a funny sound, not quite a laugh. 'Carmel.'

Rose takes a deep breath.

'Each student has his own personal body to dissect. Takes all year,' Jean says, stirring a teaspoon of sugar into her tea. 'Of course they have to learn … but just imagine.'

Rose sips her tea. 'My eldest sister's name was Carmel. She had to look after us all when Mum died. Eight of us. I was only three.'

'You poor dear,' Jean says. 'Losing those babies. Then Tom's accident … on top of all the trouble he caused.'

Rose kneads the soft white flesh of her arms; her flesh bruises easily. Tom had crinkly eyes, as blue as the sky. 'Such a nice man,' she told Carmel, when Tom asked her to marry him.

'And then Donnie,' Jean adds.

Rose's cup clatters on her saucer. She can feel her mouth tightening.

Jean fetches more hot water for the teapot. 'What I mean is poor Donnie can't have a normal life, can he?' she says. Some of the water splashes onto the table.

Rose's chin juts towards Jean. 'He got an A for his last essay. His teacher says he has a real appreciation of literature.'

'That's very good,' Jean says, her hand smoothing the damp spot on the tablecloth.

Rose stares at Jean's hand, motionless now on the white linen. 'Where do they get the bodies?' she asks, looking at the cupboards behind Jean's head.

Jean gapes at her.

'I mean the bodies the students dissect,' Rose says.

Jean shrugs. 'I think people donate their bodies to the university.'

'Will you want the body back?' The man at the Department of Anatomy and Cell Biology has a deep voice. 'I mean, will your family want the body back?'

'No, no, no,' Rose says, twisting the phone cord around her arm. 'We won't want it back.' She giggles. It sounds so funny.

'Afterwards, the university arranges for the cremation of the body at a time and place of its choice.' The man sounds as if he's reading from a form.

'Oh good,' Rose says. That's the point. 'I don't want any body left.' There is a small pause. She imagines the man tugging at his tie, though probably he isn't wearing one. Men don't always wear ties now.

He clears his throat and goes on about what a noble thing she is doing. For the good of humanity, he says. An important contribution to medical knowledge. 'Shall I send out the forms to you?'

'Oh, yes, please,' she says. She gives him her address. Such a nice man. She giggles again. Another of Rose's nice men! The first one had brown eyes and a silky moustache.

She must have been about four, sitting on the back steps, the sun warm on her face, listening to her big sister clattering pots and pans in the kitchen.

Carmel called out that she was to run up to the corner shop and get some more milk. 'Be quick about it. Dad will be home for lunch today.' Rose pulled a face but hoisted herself slowly from the steps.

She took a shortcut home across the paddock so that Carmel wouldn't be cross. A man was leaning against the big peppercorn tree, a nice man with a silky moustache and brown eyes. 'Want some lollies?' he asked.

'Wait a minute,' Rose said. She ran, the milk slopping from side to side, some splashing over the lip.

She plonked the billy and the change on the bench.

'Go and wash your hands,' Carmel said.

'In a minute. There's a nice man up the paddock. He's going to buy me some lollies.'

Carmel grabbed her shoulder. 'Oh no, you don't.' Rose struggled, but Carmel was too strong. 'Men who promise lollies take you away in a sack, and cut you into little pieces, and no-one ever sees you again,' Carmel said, shaking her.

Rose laughs until her eyes water. She dabs them with her handkerchief. What would Carmel say now? Cut into little pieces; and no one will ever see her again.

She closes her eyes. The new kitchen will be lovely: cupboards and benches of warm golden wood; only the sink will be stainless steel.

Requiem mass can still be said. She wants that. Rose imagines the priest's voice … *Thy mercy may make her the companion of the holy Angels in heaven. Through Christ our Lord.*

Donnie and Wendy and her four will sit in the front pews. Maybe some great grandchildren, too. Jean will do the flowers. But there will be no coffin.

An Exact Science

Deidre Ryan

There's the flickering light of a candle under the door before I hear the knock.

'Louisa Collins, get yourself dressed.'

I manoeuvre myself into the scratchy dress that every prisoner here wears, blood beating in my ears.

When Mrs Brown enters, her candle transforms my cell into its familiar patchwork of grey – the sandstone that keeps me in, the dress I wear, the single cup and bowl I was issued, and the aged straw mattress on the ground. The lone colour is the glistening green branches that have been inching over one wall as I sleep, a mould bloom that will be my only funeral shroud.

She squeezes my arm and I lean into the warmth, breathing in lavender, wax and something pleasantly yeasty, like bread. 'It's Sunday, love. You must know it can't happen today.'

She's a bit of a gate, Mrs Brown – not much can get around her. It's what makes her so good at the job. She sees your thoughts bubbling away and snuffs the flame before you even knew they were on the hob.

'It'll happen Tuesday … or maybe not at all.' She looks away. We both know a pardon isn't likely. 'Sorry, pet, Nosey Bob's orders,' she says, binding my wrists.

'Afraid of a woman, is he?' This is how Mrs Brown likes me. Spirited, bordering on cheeky. But Nosey Bob having orders for me is a bad sign. I know better than to ask where I'll be taken tonight.

She's still giggling when he arrives.

'Mrs Brown, I trust everything is in order?' Even after the stories, his face is worse than I could've imagined. His way of speaking is not what I expected either. He has the airs of someone above his station and a dark suit to match. Something about the way he holds his body says he used to be a looker too, before the horse's hoof took the nose clean off his face. They say his cab company was well-liked by the ladies of Sydney before that. If I was a gambling woman, I'd bet he took those ladies for a ride, all right.

He nods to Mrs Brown and strides out. I follow, flanked by two guards, my rustling hem on the stone floor the only noise apart from our steps.

My boots peek out with each pace. May, my only girl of ten babes, used to pretend my boots were kittens hiding beneath my skirts. *Peek-a-boo! I-see-you,* she'd say to my feet as we walked. I thought of drawing eyes and whiskers on the toes one day, just to delight her, but I never got around to it. Eleven now, I doubt she even remembers that.

She's a bruise I can't stop pressing since they brought me here. My fingers always seeking out the shadows, pushing down on the memories so they can't fade.

There are corridors leading into other corridors, filled with the cloying fug of damp, until we spill out of the gaol's bowels.

How can I say what it's like to see the world again, after a year in a coffin seven paces by nine? I could drink the dark sky like a pint. My eyes jerk around my skull, at the silver-tinted gums fragrant and crackling in the wind above, at the thistles crushed under my heel, oozing fresh green. The dark air is heady with an oncoming storm. I guzzle it: greedy and loud and shameless. Everything is so alive.

It must be late — we've got the street pretty much to ourselves. By the lantern's trembling light, I steal glances at the three men. My mama always said not to find myself alone with men in the dark. Not that I ever paid her much mind. There's dead silence, and then the rush and clatter of hooves on stone. Two prison carriages stop before us.

Nosey Bob is speaking to me, only I can't hear what he is saying. He waves at the first carriage, his movements tufts of clouds; the guards, the horses, everything is blurring at the edges, losing shape. I stumble and the horses rears as I land on the still-hot stones. A guard bends over me, delivering a brusque hard slap. 'No nonsense, Louisa.' Thick bodies pull me up, crowding me into the first carriage.

The door locks behind me. I am alone.

I don't want to be alone in the dark again. There are no windows, nothing to look at. The deprivation is worse now than it was in my cell, because of what I have seen, what I have remembered. I listen for signs of where we are going, but there's only thundering hooves and the low growl of the wind.

When the door opens again, rotting hits me — acrid and hostile on the nose. The three men are watching me; Nosey Bob says we're at an abattoir on Glebe Island, though I cannot guess why and he will not tell.

I'm ushered inside a liver-coloured brick building; there's a metallic taste in the air. As we move deeper, the high-pitched howling of flies fills my ears. When we stop, the flickering lantern throws shadows around the room until I can't tell the difference between my nightmares and reality. All the tools of death hang along the length of the wall – hammers, hooks, every kind of knife imaginable. Panic rises with the sick in my throat, the sharp edges opening up every cut I've had in my life.

I follow Nosey Bob towards a scale, our steps muffled by the forgotten flesh caked on the grating floor. He nods to the scale's platform but I can't move. A guard steps forward, pushing me into place. Already cattle.

'What people don't understand, Louisa my dear, is that a hanging is an exact science,' Nosey Bob says, fiddling with the scale.

Nosey Bob is, in fact, known across New South Wales for cocking up that *exact science*. Like the four men condemned to hang together a few years back. The papers said no one in the crowd pitied them as they struggled and screamed, not after what they did to that little girl, though plenty a hard man lost his lunch as he watched.

'Physics, my dear. It's all a matter of physics. The rope needs to be just the right length for your weight. Too short and you'll strangle slowly. Too long and we've got a decapitation on our hands. We don't want that for your pretty neck now, do we?' He pauses to look at me. 'Even if you are a husband killer, *twice* over.'

I suck in a breath and my hand moves to my mouth. So, you aren't the bungler, the papers say. How easily you could make me die slowly, gasping.

I give him my blank look – I have a good one, it's certainly been well-practised this past year – and think of all I would say to him if we had met at the pub instead of here. Wouldn't that be delicious?

🕊

The problem was the drinking. Mr Lusk, my solicitor, said we could've told a different story if not for the drinking – and what the drinking led to. He blushed when he said that. After all the things that have been said about me, I couldn't help but love him for it.

I'm a fast woman, you see. I like to dance. I like to drink. I liked dancing and drinking more than I liked my first husband, Charles. More than I liked being a mother. More than I liked anything before I met Michael.

Living with Charles was twenty years of shouting down a well – I could scream anything I wanted down at my life, but no one would hear it. Not my dour old husband or the endless babies he put in me.

You can't blame me for taking a drink or two. For wanting more of that fire in your belly and wings on your soul. To believe, however fleetingly, that life could be different.

I was three brandies into the evening when Michael walked into the Amos Pier Hotel. If you'd have seen me there, you would've done up another button on your blouse. I felt like a pot of caramel on the fire: hot and sticky and ready to be devoured. Michael had never tasted something so sweet.

So, I wasn't sorry when Charles was dead. Not one jot. But if I could go back to that moment, I'd pretend I was. Because that's when the trouble began.

It's all dark, the witching hour. Though he's gone, the holes in Nosey Bob's face where his nose ought to be stare at me from the black of my cell.

I close my eyes, open them again, concentrate on breathing as deep and regular as I'm able. The air is close, fetid from the unemptied slops pail and the high mercury.

I picture Michael – my only salve. The deep creases around his eyes when he laughed. His long hands, too beautiful for the woolsheds. His taste of smoke and salt and honey. But soon the memories sour, like milk in the heat. Like they always do. It's his face the day he came home early, looking off kilter. How he kept saying, 'I'll be up in a few days,' until the last.

The inquest and trials jerk through my mind like an ill-practised song, stopping and replaying moments over and over, until they come to May on the stand that last time. She looked so much like Charles up there, sharp nose and pale hair, lips curled in her disappointment with me. She'd never belonged to him more than in that moment.

The prosecutor leaned towards her, voice humming low and concerned. 'May, did your stepfather Michael Collins drink alcohol?'

'Yes sir, I was often sent down to the pub for him.'

'And your mother, did she drink?'

Even before she answered, a cold dread soaked my heart through. You can imagine, I reckon, what the papers had said about my drinking. 'Do you know what they see when they look at you, Louisa?' Mr Lusk had said. 'They see the *lush* of Botany. Two dead husbands. *Their* wife spooning rat poison into *their* tea. Show them that you are not those things.' I hung my head like he had said to.

'Yes, sir,' May said. 'Brandy. Though she'll even drink ale, if there's naught else to be had.'

'Tell me, May, what did they do after your father died?'

'They had a party, sir.' She swallowed around a sob. 'The whole neighbourhood up singing and dancing 'til the early morn.'

Behind me, a man hissed, 'You can't trust a merry widow or a whore,' and my cheeks flamed.

The prosecutor cleared his throat. 'Can you tell us about the box you found, please May?'

'It was Rough on Rats,' she said, her eyes misted over like someone was boiling a pot in her head.

'How can you be so sure?'

Her head snapped towards him. 'Because I saw it, sir. When Michael ailed and when my father died, too. I know what it was. It had a rat on it and I can read. R-O-U-G-H-O-N-R-A-T-S.'

Bile rose in my throat and Mr Lusk caught my eye, warning me to do and say nothing. Looking down, I realised my hands were balled into fists, the knuckles fishbone-white.

It took them less than two hours to find me guilty; it was a Saturday, they wanted to go home. There was a pause before the courtroom exploded into pockets of glee and outrage, dividing as neatly as men and women at a church picnic.

Mr Lusk put his hand over mine and I gaped at him. Silent. Obliterated. 'Louisa, it's been almost thirty years since a woman was hanged in New South Wales. The sentences are *always* commuted. It's not time to fret yet.'

He doesn't tell me that anymore. He says I'll die at the private scaffold, not the one that lies beyond the sandstone gates. They're willing to make an example of me, but not a spectacle of my twitching feet.

Now, I lean against the gaol's coarse sandstone wall, pushing myself out of the twisted nightmare. The floor is cool and solid under my feet. I plait my hair into a long braid, oily and stiff under my fingertips. I can see the grey in it. The papers made so much of the fact that I started dyeing my hair when I married Michael, that I lied about my age to seem closer to his. As though it was evidence for the jury.

I loop the plait around my neck, tightening it inch by inch – until terror pricks at my bladder – then let it drop against my chest.

I should've had a kind word for May when her father died. Maybe she wouldn't have turned against me. But I'd forgotten that she loved Charles, that anyone *could*.

She'd refused to call Michael anything but 'Collins' when he moved in. Yet she doted on him when he ailed, insisting on mixing his brandy and milk, saying I always made it curdle. I thought she was softening towards him. I didn't see it for what it was. Not even as her story hardened with each of the trials, like layers of varnish upon wood.

Was it punishment for what I did to her father? Or did she just take him because I loved him, more than I've loved anyone?

If I could go back, I'd do things different, my word I would. But all I can do now is try make it right before I swing. Letter after letter I've written, begging to see May before I die.

It'll be today or never. As I wait, I imagine closing my hands around her freckled neck. Praying she's fool enough to come. That she'll meet Lady Justice before I do.

Ash Puppies

Jennie Del Mastro

I hadn't been alone for nine years. Even when Hannah wasn't home, there were traces: socks in the corner, magazines facedown on the table, milk rings on the bench, crumbs in my books. I never succeeded in persuading her to tidy up. I cleaned but she spread out again to fill every inch of the house.

They say a change of scene helps to soothe grief. Or do they? Anyway, they're wrong. Hannah was gone, and everything else was gone too, right down to her hairs clogging the vacuum cleaner head, and the vacuum cleaner itself, the carpet, books, birds, home, world. It was a complete and comprehensive change of scene, but it didn't soothe me at all. I guess the point is distraction, and there was nothing left to distract me.

We had been sitting on the couch hand in hand, talking, when the fire came through. It passed over and around me, heat like the pleasant pain of chilli on the tongue, harmless.

The land was grey now, rippling out to the horizon, leaping into bare hills and mountains. A smell of burning hung over it, but not the cosy smell of a hearth-fire burning dead wood, scorched match ends and lost marshmallows. It was the bitter smell of a wildfire that had burnt living people and left nothing behind.

Then Lisa came skipping along the street in her school uniform, the way she did every weekday. Only now the street and the school were gone. She spotted me and came running.

'Be careful,' I said quickly, before she could ask me where Hannah was. 'You're kicking up the ash. It's all full of …' I paused, thinking how young she was.

'Dead things?' she said. 'People and animals – is that what you were going to say? It isn't, you know. They disappeared into nothing.'

'No, they didn't.'

'My mum did. And even if she didn't …' She smiled, and for a moment I had the bizarre idea that she'd caused the disaster. 'She always lets me do whatever I want.'

'I noticed.'

'I think she would say – Lisa, kick me right up to the sky if you like! Make me fly!' She kicked hard at the ash with a little grunt. It didn't reach the sky. Most of it was caught by the wind and tossed in my face.

'Thanks,' I said.

She sat down beside me, and stayed quiet and thoughtful for a while. Not sad, though. I wouldn't say sad. Her hair was beautifully, professionally cut, framing her face and ending just below her ears. It sat perfectly as children's hair sometimes does, except for one part on her left temple where the smooth wave of brown hair was disturbed. It looked like something was underneath, pushing out.

I told myself it was just a cowlick. Lots of kids have them. They weren't sinister. They were cute.

'I've got an idea for a game,' she said. 'Here, I'll show you.'

She scrambled over, carelessly scattering the ashes over my knees, and reached for my neck. I flinched, feeling her small hands on my throat, the monkey bar calluses and rough bitten nails. We stared at each other. My eyes must have looked tired and bemused. Hers were fierce. After a few minutes I realised she was trying to choke me. I hadn't breathed in all that time.

'Feel okay?' she asked, letting go.

'Fine,' I said.

'Now me.' She sat back, expectant.

'I'm not choking a kid,' I said.

She looked disappointed. 'Well, you can do this, can't you?' She covered her nose and mouth. 'If I start to struggle, you let go,' she said through her hands.

'All right.' I put one hand over her face and blocked her mouth and nose. It felt like some old spy movie. She didn't even twitch. It seemed like a long time before I let her go.

'I've drunk weed killer,' she said. 'It tasted disgusting. And I put my feet in a fire – that hurt but didn't burn me. And I jumped off the roof of our house. Maybe tomorrow we can think of something else to do. I'm stuck for ideas now everything's burned. Why didn't you use that hand?' she added, pointing to my left hand, which was clenched tight.

I shrugged.

'What are you hiding?'

'Nothing.'

She grabbed for it, but I got to my feet and held it up over my head where she couldn't reach it.

We walked for days. The ashes moved into shallow dunes, dragged by the wind. They made a thin layer of dust over us, creeping up our legs. I brushed them off but they came right back. The whole world was made of ash. I breathed it, felt it on my tongue and between my fingers.

'Poke me in the eye,' Lisa would say suddenly, and I'd spend a reluctant hour playing her weird game of trying to damage each other.

Unexpectedly, we still needed sleep. When the sun went down the first night in spectacular scarlet and orange through the haze of lingering smoke, I had to lie down and close my eyes. Maybe it was just a leftover instinct, a convention. Had I ever really needed it?

Some nights I woke to feel her peeling my fingers back. At least then I had an excuse to pull away. I didn't have to pretend my skin wasn't crawling. Then she'd go to the other side of me and cuddle up there instead.

Between loneliness and that freaky little waif, I'd choose loneliness. The most frightening thing in this wasteland was catching her glance. But I didn't have a choice. She followed me everywhere. I wondered if I was going crazy. I couldn't even say her name when I spoke.

How did I fill in time before the world ended? Clothes, I imagined. Washing them, hanging them on the line, bringing them in. Folding them, putting them away. Choosing which ones to wear, discarding them, gathering them again. Trying them on, buying them, donating them.

Now I had only what was on my back. I wondered why, of all the things in the world, my least favourite shirt and my slightly too-tight shorts had managed to survive. Would they get smelly? Would it matter? I sniffed at myself.

Lisa was watching me.

'What?' I said.

'What?' she said.

We met the man after two weeks. I blessed whatever or whoever had led us to him, saving me from a lifetime of being Lisa's only companion. We found him on his knees, digging with his hands, sweeping away ash and piling up the dirt he found underneath.

'Hello.' He looked up with sad dark eyes.

'Hello,' I said.

'Can you make her open this?' Lisa asked. She was hanging off my left hand again.

The man sat back on his heels. 'If she's saved a treasure, let her have it. I had a book in my pocket. My favourite book. Now it's ash. But my pocket is still here. What a mystery. Why do I need a pocket? Why, little girl? What can I put in it?'

Lisa let go of me and giggled. It was the first laugh I'd heard since the fire. She sat down and I did too, promising myself I would leave alone or in a trio.

'What are you doing?' she asked, watching him through narrow eyes.

Hannah wouldn't have asked. She would have told him: 'You're making dirt puppies.' And then she'd help. I curled up, hugging my legs and looking at my stomach. She called sand castles 'sand puppies'. I knew there was a reason, but I didn't want to lose myself digging too far back there.

'I used to have lots of beautiful things,' said the man. 'I was a collector. But look, now. All I have is a watch I bought at the supermarket.'

'Piles of dirt aren't beautiful either.'

'There's nothing else.'

'Except ash,' she said.

He mumbled and nodded.

The collector had made twenty-six dirt puppies so far. Lisa kept watching him. He suddenly stopped and asked her, 'Can you pray, little girl?'

'Yes,' she said.

'I'm not good at praying out loud, but I think it might be the thing to do.'

'No,' I said. 'Don't.'

'Why not?'

'Because … because God doesn't care. Otherwise he wouldn't do this. And if he wasn't powerful enough to stop it, why bother praying to him?'

'A momentous question,' said the collector. 'The search for an answer is the search of your life.'

He spoke so seriously it made me feel silly. I wasn't searching for answers. I knew what they were. All I could see was Hannah, holding my hand, praying her prayer. 'Thanks for Mummy. Thanks for being with us. Thanks for all the good things. Sorry I messed up again. Please look after Mummy. Please look after me. Please 'specially look after Mummy.'

I curled up again, and blocked my ears and closed my eyes. Lisa started murmuring. It went on for a while, then stopped. I relaxed, and saw them both looking at me.

'Sorry. I couldn't …'

'It's okay,' said Lisa.

She left me alone that night.

The next morning the collector made another row of dirt puppies. I wondered if he'd be happy to come with us. Or could I leave Lisa with him? These questions were momentous for me now. They were the only framework for my life. No job, no home, no family. Just three people and what we would do in the long days ahead.

Lisa shuffled over to the collector and clicked her fingers. A small white flame appeared, bright as burning magnesium. She was holding it in her hands with her eyes carefully averted. She rubbed her palms together and the flame grew larger. Then she leant over the nearest dirt puppy and put her hands on it. The collector stumbled out of the way, scattering several other puppies.

The pile of dirt smoked and dwindled.

'I can make another one,' said the collector.

Lisa smiled at him and smothered the flames with her hands. A hot little circle of rainbow glass lay on the ground. The collector blew on it, then picked it up, holding it to the light.

'I burned up all the other stuff in the dirt,' said Lisa, 'and melted the sand. There wasn't much.'

'Clever girl. It's beautiful. The first treasure of the new world!' He was on his feet, dancing around, humming and raising the glass to the sun.

'That's how I did it,' she said.

'Thank you! Thank you!' he said, patting her shoulder.

'I mean that's how I burned everything.'

It took me a moment to understand. 'You're joking.'

She shook her head and rubbed her fingers together. 'I lost control.'

'That's crazy.'

'You're crazy, I'm crazy, she's crazy,' said the collector. 'Everyone's crazy at the end of the world.'

She shook his arm, making him drop the glass disc. 'But I didn't burn the whole world! I just … I *singed* part of it.'

'It's the end of the world,' said the collector stubbornly, scooping up his treasure.

'It's *not*.'

She had to be imagining things. I remembered Hannah being convinced that she'd knocked down a tree at school. One day she'd leaned against the tree and heard it creak. The next day it was gone. She tearfully showed me a smooth stump that had clearly been cut by a chainsaw.

'What makes you think you did this?'

Lisa looked at me out of the corner of her eye and smiled like a devious little planet destroyer. I lost my head. I grabbed her with my right hand, turned her over on my lap and gave her five very hard smacks on the bottom. She screeched like a bird and scrambled away.

Immediately I regretted it. I had always been on the side of positive reinforcement. My friend Robyn was a hands-on-hips mother who insisted that when you didn't punish the bad, you made it the new normal. But she was in the minority. Our generation had all but outlawed corporal punishment. And this violent self-justifying little minx was all that was left of the children we had made.

Lisa turned her back on me. 'You're horrible.'

Maybe I'd done the right thing after all. I rubbed my hand on my leg. 'If your mum had done that, she might still be here.'

'*So* horrible,' she said.

Maybe I was. But the nerves in my palm were barely firing up their obsolete system. I knew Lisa wasn't in as much pain as she pretended.

Later she sidled over, quiet and humble. 'I'm sorry about burning everything. You can try and kill me if you like, as a punishment.' Then I caught the gleam in her eye. She was ready for another game.

'You know we can't do that, even if we thought it was a good idea.'

She sat at a loss for a while, then turned another dirt puppy into a glass disc, and another, and another. Soon she and the collector had their pockets jingling with treasure. She offered me one, but I shook my head.

That night it was hard to fall asleep. The earth was utterly dark, making the stars brighter than I had ever seen them. The Milky Way's shimmering dust had separated into distinct white sparkles, and the once empty blackness had produced dust of its own. The sky came down around us to the horizon on all sides. I felt like I was falling forward into it.

'There's the Southern Cross,' said Lisa.

'There's Orion,' said the collector.

'Do you know any animal stars?' asked Lisa. 'Do you know the Bear?'

'No, just the other two.'

'Are there any animals left, do you think? Any real ones?'

'We haven't seen any so far.'

She sighed heavily. 'If I knew it would be like this, I wouldn't have done it.'

'Maybe birds or insects survived by flying over the fire,' said the collector.

We'd probably find some cockroaches, I thought, but stayed silent.

'Light a fire, little girl. A moth might come.'

Lisa did. It looked like a big star come to earth, resting in her hands. 'Maybe one was hidden in an egg, protected, when the fire came past.'

'When Ha—' My throat spasmed. I stopped. My chest was constricted. Was I having a heart attack? I was half scared, half relieved. This might be the end. But the feeling slowly faded. They were both waiting. 'When Ha—'

'Hannah?' said Lisa.

'Yes. When … when she was little, she called moths "mops".'

Lisa smiled.

'Who is Hannah?' asked the collector.

I forced myself to speak. 'My daughter. Eight years old. Messy brown hair and blue eyes. Liked jokes and playing the piano.'

'She was nice,' said Lisa.

'She was your treasure,' said the collector. 'Go on.'

'One time,' I said tentatively, 'we were sitting outside a café, and a dog went past. Hannah said, "Want a crumb, puppy?" and I asked her what a crumb puppy was.'

Lisa laughed.

'We talked about what it might be. In the end we agreed it was a blob formed by squeezing crumbs together. Like a dust bunny, only it didn't live under a couch, but on your plate. It was born when you played with your food and died when you washed the dishes. Hannah pretended to be upset with me because I killed all the crumb puppies born in our house. And I pretended to be upset – because it really did bother me – that she always left the dirty work to me. Then she made a whole family of crumb puppies on her plate. After that, everything was a puppy.'

'I liked Hannah,' said Lisa. 'She was nice to me.'

The next day we started walking. The collector seemed happy to come, and stirred the treasure in his pocket. He was deferential with Lisa. I imagined it was the manner he used for his best supplier.

'In a way it's good,' he said. 'Immortality. No need for food, drink, shelter, safety. The chance for unlimited travel. On the other hand …' He looked around. 'Nothing to see.'

Early on the second morning we smelt salt and fish. Through the first hour's walking the wind grew slowly cooler. The ash began to be scattered with drips and smears that gleamed. The blue line on the horizon thickened. I waited for someone to say it, but nobody spoke, so I did.

'The sea!'

We came to a place where the hills of ash were left behind us, and the sand had been melted into glass right down to the edge of the water. It shone in the sunlight, blinding us.

'Ah!' said the collector, and threw himself on the ground, stroking the glossy ripples.

The waves lapped over the glass silently without the hush of water over sand, only a glug and a splash now and then. Maybe the fire had boiled some of the water; but not enough to dry the ocean. The destruction had stopped here.

'The sea's probably still full of fish and things,' said Lisa.

'Shells,' I said. 'Big conches and clams.'

I thought the collector would be interested but he didn't seem to hear. He was still caressing the glass, murmuring.

'Can I swim?' asked Lisa, poised on tiptoe.

'Can you drown?' I asked. 'That's the question.'

Her face lit up and she went sliding down the shiny slope, bouncing over bumps and saying 'Ow!' She ground to a halt at the edge of the water and rolled herself the rest of the way, disappearing under the waves.

'Don't go too far!'

The collector sat down beside me with a groan. 'The old world is still out there, maybe. Across the sea. We could swim there.'

'Eager to find some more treasures?'

He smiled.

'But what about Lisa?' I asked. 'We can't take her where there are normal people.'

'Do you believe she did this?'

'I don't know.'

'She'll survive on her own,' he said hesitantly, then caught my eye. 'Yes. That is not kind. But I don't want to go back there.' He pointed inland. 'And they will find us anyway, one day.'

'We need to keep moving, until she's older. We'll know her better by then. Maybe we'll work out what really happened.'

'We could follow this beautiful glass along the coast. Yes. Let's.'

Lisa popped up and yelled, 'I breathed in water! I didn't drown! I didn't even cough!'

'That's good!'

'And I'm clean!' she said, sticking out her arms. 'The ash is all gone!'

My left hand was still closed over my treasure. I couldn't carry it like this forever. Maybe I should lose it in the sea. Hannah loved the sea. Or I could let it blow away in the wind. She always wanted to fly, herself, not in a plane. But most of all she liked being tucked away somewhere, cosy and safe.

'Lisa!' I shouted.

She came slipping on the slick glass, using the irregularities as hand holds to pull herself up.

'Can you make me a tiny bowl of glass? Please?'

'Okay!' she said brightly. She rubbed her fingers together until they were red hot and softened the glass near her knees, pulling out a lump of it, stretching the transparent strands like mozzarella until they gave way and flopped over in a petrified wave.

'Beautiful,' said the collector.

Lisa lit her fingers on fire and shaped the lump of glass into a little glowing ball. Then she handed it to me.

It cooled and hardened as I touched it. I opened my left hand with a gasp of relief, my fingers stiff and creaking, and poured the ashes into the hollow she had made. They stuck to my palm, but I dusted them off gently with a finger. Lisa was busy forming a lid. When it was done, she fused it over the top of the bowl, heating and moulding it until it was a smooth marble. I rolled it in my hands, kissed it and then pulled off my shoes and poked it down into one of the toes.

Lisa giggled.

'Thank you,' I said, and I brushed the wet hair back from her forehead. 'Come on.'

The three of us slid down the hard, shiny beach, slipping in the waves. A few steps out, I felt soft sand under my feet. Seaweed tangled around my ankles. Here the fire had never reached. Here there was life. I felt a rip tug at me, and I let it catch me and pull me out deep under the surface.

The Family Tradition

Zena Shapter

I don't want to see my daughter weighing lettuce, but there she is at the kitchen bench with the scales. I blink, rehear my husband's words from last night, and force myself to watch. Iceberg, cos, restaurant mix, butterhead – it won't matter what she adds, the calorie count will be the same. Negligible. Still, she believes the figures will all add up in that little diary of hers, the one she thinks I don't know about, and that's all that matters to the Rachel standing before me. I don't know how she could ever imagine I'd be oblivious to her plans. Then again, she doesn't know I made her who she is: a young woman, weighing salad the day before her wedding. Women rarely realise how much of a role model their mums were for them, unless and until they become mothers themselves.

Rachel, therefore, may never know.

After removing the lettuce she weighs the tomatoes. Her shoulder blade pinches at the insides of her skin as she balances the scales. I remember the beautiful skin she had as a baby, so soft I'd press my face into her cheeks, her tummy. All I see when I look at this girl is a skeleton moving under a transparent pink coat. She's lucky we live in the cool mountain air and tomorrow she can hide her arms inside a lace wrap. They're getting married deep underground too, in a cave at Jenolan, where sharp stalactites will distract guests from her similarly pointed elbows. What kind of man marries a girl like this anyway?

'Are we seeing Alex today?' I ask her.

She frowns while slicing the cucumber. Trouble concentrating, I know that feeling well. It comes hand-in-hand with giddiness during your morning shower, and holding on tight when climbing stairs in case your muscles give way underneath you. It wasn't the falling I ever dreaded, but the possibility that my own secret plans might be discovered. I thought I was invisible too, like Rachel. I thought my family believed me when I said I'd already eaten. Now I'm not sure. It's seems so obvious now, from where I'm watching.

'Um.' Rachel finally stops slicing. 'He'll pop in later, I think, to pick up the rings.'

'So he's not staying tonight?'

'No,' she says, scoffing. 'Of course not. He's staying with his parents.' Rachel has always accepted traditions for what they are, no questions asked. Maybe that's why she's bound to turn out like me.

'And what about you?' I ask. 'Going out?'

'No!' There's an edge to her voice now. She needs to eat. 'I've got way too much to do, Mum.' She huffs and starts slicing again.

Were my mood swings that noticeable?

'Of course you do, darling.' I don't know why I even asked. I know exactly what she'll be doing tonight. After all, she is my daughter. She'll jog on the spot in front of her bedroom mirror while everyone else watches television downstairs, just because she ate a chocolate at her rehearsal dinner. She'll do sit-ups and floor exercises until she feels faint. She might even swoon. Then she'll have to stop, and she'll despair that she hasn't done enough to look good for her big day, that she won't look as beautiful as her friends. She'll examine herself in the mirror but won't see her bony chest or meatless legs. She'll only see the wobble around her middle. Her friends all have flat tummies, whereas hers bulges with the thin layer of fat that her body's desperately storing until the famine it perceives changes to abundance. Yes, I know how it is and how it will be.

Her friends would have told her countless times they're jealous of her body's natural curves, at least the ones she used to have. She'll never believe them, just as I never did mine. And I'll never know the exact moment she became destined to follow in my footsteps. Only hints and clues clarified with hindsight and acceptance will tell me after it's too late. I might catch her staring at the reverse of cereal packets or bread bags, assessing the calorie counts, but she'll say she's looking for the best-before date. I might catch her eyeing pictures of models in magazines, examining their individual flaws and perfections, but she'll say she's looking for the clothing suppliers' details. And I'll want to believe her, because then I won't have to change.

If only I could blame the media, peer pressure, or her friends … If they took responsibility, I wouldn't have to blink again. But I do, because I know my husband is right.

So there Rachel is again, and this time I see her at sixteen. She's stopped having periods for a year now and we're taking her for a full medical check-up. The doctor says there's nothing wrong with her, apart from being a little thin.

'Thin?' Rachel scoffs.

'You don't think you're thin, Rachel?' The doctor twigs. 'Which part of you then do you think is fat?'

She looks at him as if the answer is obvious, then rethinks and lowers her eyes.

When it was me sitting in the doctor's chair, I wasn't as clever, as careful.

'All of me,' I'd said, instantly realising my mistake. My husband hadn't had a clue until then. He thought my body was doing something weird after giving up breastfeeding. He suspected the problem was hormonal, that my body simply didn't know when to stop using up the fat it had stored during pregnancy, like my friends said it would, even though I'd breastfed Rachel for her first twelve months. No, my husband thought the reason I wasn't having periods, and why we couldn't conceive again yet, was because of some kind of imbalance.

But of course Rachel is— would be cleverer than me. She would have had years of practice and an impeccable teacher. After all, this is a family tradition now.

'My bum,' she tells the doctor.

He makes her strip and turn around so he can give her an honest opinion. He's not being a pervert, he's trying to help her, like my doctor tried to help me.

'If you keep going this way,' he warns Rachel, as my doctor warned me, 'you'll make yourself infertile.'

Silly man. I had only one thought when my doctor said I looked fine to him. Rachel says the same thing as we leave: 'What does he know?'

You can't tell people like us that we look good. It's not something we can believe. We don't even think we're really loved by anyone, merely tolerated. We're not worthy of love.

So no kids or siblings for Rachel and no grandchildren for me. This is the choice we have to make – our fertility or our beauty. Will Rachel choose to live for her future, or follow the path I've shown her?

She would have caught me a million times already, examining myself in the hallway mirror, the mirrors of fitting rooms and car-window reflections, a look of disgust on my face. She would have seen me skip lunch, skip dinner, drink only nutrition shakes for breakfast. She would have seen me step off the scales to remove my top, then step back on again. She would have grown up thinking this was normal, that this was how women stayed thin, beautiful.

I shake my head at the images I'm seeing, but whether I close my eyes to blink or not, a thirteen-year-old Rachel now stands before me.

'Can we go shopping this weekend, Mum?' She

hunches and readjusts her waistband. She stands awkwardly, sits awkwardly. I understand her pain. Today's clothes are all aimed at boy-bottoms and bony hips, of which she has neither. Gone are the days when fashion flattered a grown woman's true curves. All they do now is make sticks look feminine and call them girls.

So maybe it's the media's fault after all? I could blame fashion journalism for us both?

I sigh and blink again. Rachel is seven now.

'Mummy, this t-shirt is broken.'

It isn't broken. Her top is stiff so it sticks out over her round belly. She pulls it down. There's still a gap where the cold air could blow up inside. They should make waistbands higher. Then again, I'm sure my imagination would only create another body issue for little seven-year-old Rachel. After all, she is destined to turn out like me.

Isn't she?

I rub my eyes to see morning light on the blinds and sit up in bed. I've had enough of visualising my daughter's future. Right now she's still four years old, asleep in the bedroom next to ours, safe and happy. Nothing is set in stone.

'Lead by example,' my husband John begged me yesterday as we left the doctor's, where I stripped and listened to his honest opinion about my not being fat. 'Please, Mia. What if Rachel becomes like you? Can you imagine how awful you'd feel if she started copying you?'

Lying here awake now for hours, it's all I have been imagining – Rachel as a bride, as a teenager, at thirteen, at seven …

My stomach growls. The gnawing hunger sends a ripple of euphoric pleasure through me. My body isn't getting enough calories, which means it isn't getting fatter, only thinner. I like the sensation. No, I love it. It makes me feel good, powerful. What Rachel said yesterday was probably a one-off.

While I was at the doctor's hearing all about my potential infertility, she fell over a climbing balance at preschool. She skidded across the soft-fall and scraped her nose and upper lip. The scratches are so deep it will take weeks for them to heal. She was still crying when we collected her, though not because of the pain.

'I want them gone!' she shouted through her tears. 'I want to be pretty again. No one will like me!'

'Don't be silly,' I told her. 'Your friends won't stop liking you because of a few scratches. You share your toys, compromise all the time, and never call names. You're a great friend! Besides, they'll heal very soon.'

But now John's afraid she'll end up with other childhood scars, ones that won't fade.

'We're having photos tomorrow,' she wailed. 'And now I'm ugly!'

I don't even know where she learnt that word. I might have felt ugly, but I've never said it aloud. John can't blame me for that one.

I creep out of bed and tiptoe into Rachel's bedroom. She's cuddling her fluffy doggy tight in her little arms. I stroke her soft cheek and my tummy grumbles again. I take a deep breath and, as I expand my lungs, my stomach tightens. This is what I want for myself – firmness, flatness. I hate feeling bloated and flabby. When I look good, I feel good and I'm happy. Why should I feel guilty for wanting to be happy? Yes, I am a mother. But I'm me too. Must I sacrifice everything for my child? She's her own person. She might choose to become the exact opposite of her mother. I'm told teenagers often do.

No, I can't give this up. The minute I stop watching my weight, I'll become a big fat porker again, and not just because of the calories. John wants a little brother or sister for Rachel.

But I like being able to see my feet. I like feeling as light as a breeze. I can't go through all that again.

A buzzing noise. It's John's alarm.

Rachel stirs and opens her eyes.

'Morning.' I smile at her.

She gives me a thought-free instinctive grin that broadens until it cracks a scab on her lip. Her eyes widen with fear. 'They're not gone?'

'No, darling. I said it would take a while, remember?'

'But I haven't touched them.'

'Good, because otherwise you'll scar. Come on, let's get you dressed.'

Naturally she wants to wear her best party dress and for once I don't argue. She's not actually going to preschool today, it's not her usual day. We're only popping in for the photo shoot.

While she gets dressed, I have a shower, complete with the familiar wooziness.

John's fallen back to sleep by the time I finish, but the creaking as I slide open my wardrobe door wakes him.

'What time is it?'

'Time to get up.'

He looks at the clock. 'You were up before the alarm.'

'I wanted a big breakfast. I'm not sure where in the photo queue she'll be.' I hurry into the kitchen and put a clean plate and bowl in the sink, along with a spoon and knife, then splash them with cold water so they look rinsed. What's the harm when Rachel can't even see me? Maybe that's the solution? I need to be more careful. I switch on the kettle to make Rachel's Weet-bix. She's watching cartoons in the lounge.

'How do you want your hair?' I ask her, passing into the bathroom to fetch her hairbrush.

She shrugs, her expression grumpy.

I tie her hair into a ponytail, her favourite. 'Is that good?'

No answer.

On our way to preschool, her mood doesn't improve. She's near the front of the photo list too, so still grumpy when the photographer calls her name. She stomps to the chair and plonks herself down with a huff. He makes jokes and pulls faces. She doesn't smile. Instead her fingers go to her lip and trace the raised bumpiness of scabs.

I wink at the photographer and try bribery. 'Come on, darling. Show us your gorgeous smile.' She looks away. 'If you're good, I might buy you a *small* treat after.'

She considers this for a moment. 'A milkshake, at The View, not at home?'

I nod. 'If that's what you want.'

She nods back and smiles. The photographer clicks. As Rachel stands and makes her way back to me, I realise I just agreed to use food as a reward. Probably another thing I shouldn't be doing. 'Unless you'd prefer a toy?'

'You said I could have a milkshake!'

'Okay, okay. Let's go then.' At least she doesn't think milkshakes are evil. Clearly I've been over-imagining the situation. So has John.

'No sibling package?' the photographer asks, glancing at his clipboard.

I shake my head and rush Rachel away before she asks again when she'll get a little brother or sister, like the rest of her friends. She's on the same page as her daddy. Thankfully she's too distracted by the allure of our destination. Our local café is a short walk along the ridge.

Rachel grins at the barista as she orders. 'Two banana milkshakes, please.'

'Two?' I ask her.

'One for me, one for you.' She smiles up at me. 'Oh, unless you don't want to go for a run later,' she adds.

'What do you mean?'

'You run every time you have a treat, that's why Daddy reads me my bedtime story. Can you read to me tonight though?' She glances at the barista making the milkshakes, then directs her big brown eyes back at me. 'I'll have that for my treat instead.'

'Um.' Did she really just say what I think she said? She's noticed I jog after treats? The room sways so I reach for the counter. I blink to regain my focus and see my little Rachel shoot up before me, passing through seven, thirteen, sixteen and into a bony pale bride. My stomach heaves though there's nothing in it to spew. Only the thud of two milkshakes arriving on the counter jolts me back to reality, where my darling little girl is young again. 'You can have both, sweetheart,' I tell her, handing over the money. 'Milkshake *and* story.'

With a wide grin she reaches for her drink and I realise I want nothing in this world other than to protect and love her. She's delicious and I want a million more of her.

We find a table by the window. Verdant forest clings to the plunging lemon ravines beneath us. The yellow milk before me looks as lethal. After taking a long sip through her straw, Rachel looks expectantly at me. I lean towards my tall glass and, straw between lips, suck a tiny sip. It's sweet and frothy.

'You won't get too fat, will you?' Rachel's expression is of genuine concern.

I shake my head, both in disappointment at her casual acceptance of my routines and to answer her question. I don't want her ever repeating my traditions. I lean towards her and feel as if a haze that's kept me prisoner for years is clearing. 'You don't get fat from one treat, darling,' I tell her, I tell myself; and I take another sip to prove it. Maybe this milkshake will actually help me get fat, so fat I can't see my feet anymore and my skin stretches tight over some budding bulge that kicks and rolls, and brings me another child as breathtaking as this one?

'Good.' Rachel's feet swing under her chair. 'I love you, Mummy.'

I smile, believing her. 'I love you too. Cheers.' We chink our glasses and, even though I know I'm consuming vast quantities of calories, I am also happy. Happy because my daughter is going to be cleverer than me, more content than me. And I'm going to ensure that happens by developing some new traditions, just for her.

Out of the Forest, Into the Trees

Doug Pender

When Deacon left the office early he was already tired and bitter at missing out again on the finance director's job. Late afternoon had the sun bearing down, making his eyes flicker with sun spots. He turned the corner into his home street, the light filtered by the tall, bushy trees lining the street on both sides.

Immediately dread tightened his stomach as it always did. The Craddock mansion loomed up, behind the high rock wall pockmarked with bullet holes. Months now since the drive-by shooting but the holes had been left without repair, like an in-your-face testament to the violence brought to the street by that family.

If only he and Mary had known before they'd bought the house further down. Ahead he spotted several cars. Dark. Expensive. Parked at random angles outside the Craddock's gate. He pulled wide to get clear of them. For an instant the last rays of sun flashed across his windscreen. He blinked hard, heard a panicked scream. Felt a heavy thud under the car. He screeched the car to a stop in the middle of the road. He'd seen nothing.

In the rearview mirror, in the shadow, about six metres behind, lay a lump about the size of a large dog. A vicious fist took hold of his solar plexus and squeezed hard. Then he spotted a couple with a dog, on the side opposite the gate, all three standing transfixed, staring at the lump.

He burst out of the driver's door, desperate he'd hit nothing but a garbage bag, not one of Craddock's guard dogs. The sun had almost gone; the shadows deepened. He ran back to the shape lying in the road. When he reached it his legs gave out. He slumped to his knees alongside what was clearly a child, a boy, about eight years old, arms and legs sprawled at strange angles, eyes open in a look of shocked, frozen surprise. Deacon wanted to scream, wanted to die, wanted to be anywhere but there. He thought of running but stopped himself, not sure his legs would support him.

Then he heard the woman on a mobile phone asking for an ambulance, the man repeating over and over, 'He came out of nowhere, you couldn't have seen him, he was running from something.' They both looked over at the gate. Partly ajar. 'You better hope the ambulance and police arrive first,' the man added.

The coroner absolved Thomas Deacon of any blame, ruling it tragic but purely accidental.

When the verdict came he needed the steadying hand of the cop Ray Shandon. He felt huge gratitude for those witnesses.

Outside the inquest four police officers formed a barrier around Deacon. More than twenty men and women ringed the courtyard, black-clad, some in leather jackets, most stony faced, the women tearful, the mood thick with threat. Shandon led Deacon towards a police van. The black-clad crowd formed behind them. Then the crowd parted and through it came a man, tall, with hulking shoulders, heavy face riddled with the scars of a boxer's trade, a deep red birthmark alongside his left eye, a face familiar from news broadcasts and newspaper photo shots.

He stopped a metre from Deacon. No expression. Did not blink.

'You killed Paul. My little guy.'

'Easy, Craddock,' Shandon said.

'You heard the coroner, Mr Craddock. An accident. Nothing I could do. He ran out of nowhere.' Sweat trickled down Deacon's cheeks and under his armpits.

'You killed him.'

In a flat tone. As though he'd not even heard.

Shandon waited until Deacon pulled into the driveway. They could see Mary waiting at the lounge window, her face strained.

'We have to get you away somewhere safe, where he can't find you. With people like Craddock it's an eye for an eye, no matter how it happened.'

Shandon's blunt words pounded Deacon's tired mind. The guilt that ravaged his nights and stalked his dreams was bad enough. Now this.

'For how long? What about my job, my kids? Kate, she's in the top netball team. Jason's in the school band, performing in the end of year concert. Mary's got her own business, just taken on new staff.'

Shandon laid a consoling arm around Deacon's shoulders.

'Thomas, I understand, but as long as he knows where you are, you're all in danger. We can't protect you full time. You have to go into hiding.'

No proper sleep for days made his thinking flicker like a failing light bulb. How could he tell Mary, persuade the kids to give up everything, to understand?

As he wove along the forest tracks in the early morning the birds were his only companions. Around him bellbirds rang their chorus, whipbirds snapped, magpies chortled, crows cried like babies. Deacon felt the natural rhythm of his running blend with the sounds of the forest. He sucked in the mingled scents of gum trees and lingering astringent smells of recent burn-offs. Six months since he and his family had moved there and the sense of freedom and safety had at last begun to feel reassuring.

The scream silenced the birds and brought him to a sudden halt – the most awful sound he'd ever heard, so primal even the trees seemed to hiss. It had come from about two hundred metres away, behind that large stand of trees. He dropped to a crouch while his senses worked with desperate haste. He picked up moaning sounds and muffled voices. Definitely behind those trees. He fought the urgent flight signals, to turn, to run, breathed deep to calm his raging nerves, spotted part of a track he could use to get closer without noise. Plenty of cover, too. He swallowed his fear and moved with slow, silent steps. The moans and voices became louder and shapes formed through the branches. His vision cleared and he moved behind a large gum tree and stood rigid against it. He had a line of sight now on a small clearing and a man on his knees. His left hand clutched the stump of his right arm, trying to stem a copious flow of blood.

In the shadows beyond the clearing Deacon picked out two shapes. His throat felt tight, his body rigid to the point of numbness. If he had to run he wouldn't be able to. He could do nothing but watch, hoping, praying he wouldn't make a sound and no one would look his way.

One of the shapes came towards the cowering figure, a tall man, stooped, his face a mess of sagging jowls. In one hand he held a long, blood streaked sword. The other figure, shorter, skinnier, younger, also moved into the light. He looked scared. However, instead of inflicting further violence, the tall man shrugged at the moaning figure, turned and walked away. The younger man followed, down a path on the side opposite to where Deacon was hiding. Deacon let go a deep breath but remained deathly still. The kneeling figure screamed after the departing men.

'Don't leave me. I'll bleed to death. Please!'

Soon Deacon heard the sounds of an engine starting, a car driving away, and the hopeless sobbing of the figure now curled in a foetal position. The birds remained silent.

Some minutes elapsed before Deacon could climb on top of his shock enough to move. Even then he moved with furtive steps from cover to cover towards the figure. His mind swirled. *Run like hell, you bloody fool. Get the fuck out. It's none of your business. What if they come back?* But he couldn't back away. No matter how scary the situation, the man needed his help.

When he reached the man's side Deacon found him unconscious. He tore off his T-shirt and ripped it into strips, used one as a tourniquet, another to bandage the stump. He had to get help for him. He ran down the track to the road on wobbly legs. The forest seemed to have drawn a deep breath.

He heard the sound of a motor from around the bend. His first instinct was to plunge back into the bush. What if it was them? But he took a chance, stayed and waved when the car rounded the corner. A black Mercedes. The car came alongside and the driver's window whispered its way down. Only then did it occur to Deacon what a sight he must be. Half naked, bloody hands.

The driver stared at him. Deacon saw a lined face, deep set dark blue eyes, hair iron grey. A gravelly voice asked: 'What's the trouble?'

Deacon struggled to catch his breath. 'In the woods there ... man badly hurt ... half his arm cut off ... two men with a sword ... bleeding badly.'

'Two men with a sword?'

'Yes, but they've gone.'

'Show me.'

He led the driver back to the man who lay motionless. The driver bent, felt for a pulse in the neck.

'He's alive.'

Then he reached down, gathered up the severed limb and laid it on the man's chest. Deacon took hold of the man's legs and together they got him to the car. When the man was settled in the back seat, the driver said, 'Go home and forget what you've seen. I'll get him to hospital.'

'You sure?'

'You have a wife and family?'

'Yes.'

'All the more reason not to be involved. Go. I'll take care of it.'

Guilt ripped at Deacon but he couldn't risk exposure. He had to go. He ran off down the road and along the rest of the track, full out with the adrenalin pumping. Only then did he realise the driver hadn't introduced himself or asked Deacon his name or details.

He told her everything. She said nothing but her violet eyes stayed wide throughout. She clutched a tea towel. By the time he'd finished she'd mangled it.

'Jesus, what happened to you?' Mary dropped the laundry basket, children's clothes tumbling out onto the timbered floor. 'Tom, stop. Breathe, come on ... one ... two ... three ... Slow down and start at the beginning.'

'Who was that man in the car?'

'I don't know. Never seen him before.'

'What about the T-shirt you left behind? The one you used for the bleeding?'

'Just an old white one.'

'Oh, Tom, we can't say anything to anyone about this.'

'There's nothing to tie us to it, to anything. Mary, I only did what I had to.'

'Do you think it's got anything to do with ...?'

'No, no, it can't have. Only chance I was there.' Then it occurred to him. 'It should be on the news tonight. They're bound to report someone being found with half an arm off. It may say who did it and why. The police could even have those men already.'

'You're not thinking of testifying?'

'No. I'm not going to say anything.'

'That's if the man in the car doesn't say anything. What if he knows who you are and tells the police and they come and you've said nothing? What if they tie it in with the other?'

Neither of them wanted to name it. The helpless fear still lurked there, below the surface, ready to burst into blind panic.

Mary's voice began to shake. 'What if the man dies? They might think you did it.'

'Why would I have done it? Are you saying I could have done it?'

'I'm not saying you did it. I'm scared, that's all.'

He put his arms around her, hugged her tight. 'Darling. I had to help him. I couldn't walk away.'

'Tom, I'm scared we'll get in even more trouble.'

'Mary, if I go to the police and those men find out we could be in much worse trouble. We can't afford any attention on ourselves. It's not the police I'm worried about.'

Somehow they got through the day. The children stayed out playing with new friends at another cabin through the trees. No mention came on the radio. The first TV news at 5:30 had nothing about it, or the 6 o'clock news. Surely the ABC would have something, but no.

The children returned, full of their adventures,

needing attention, but Deacon couldn't get his mind free to listen to what they were saying. He saw Mary turning away, biting her lip. Kate looked hurt and bewildered. Jason kicked a soccer ball across the floor and demanded food. Mary screamed at him. She didn't often do that.

The children were in bed asleep and Deacon was slumped in an armchair when he realised Mary was standing over him, trembling.

'Tom, I can't stand not knowing. You have to talk to the police, find out what happened, what they're doing about it. If we don't deal with it we'll always be running. Get your jacket on and go.'

When Deacon climbed the steps of the red brick building close to midnight, the station was in chaos with the aftermath of a violent gate-crashing. Drunken yells and snarls of protest battled shouts of 'shut up', 'move over there', 'take him away', 'answer the question' from harassed police officers. A dozen or more people, mostly youths, some parents, jostled with officers.

Deacon slipped onto a bench in a corner. He'd wait. No way did he want to get caught up in that mess. Fumes of alcohol, sweat, vomit and urine swirled around him. One by one the youths were processed and either told to go or ushered to the cells at the back of the station. One burly youth took a swing and it took three officers to pin him down.

The station began to quieten and Deacon stood to approach the desk. He was halfway when a group of plainclothed police came through a door behind the desk, arguing in low voices. Deacon hunched back onto the bench, ducking his head down in a desperate bid for invisibility. The driver who'd relieved Deacon of responsibility seemed to be the one in charge.

A police officer. What was going on? Every one of Deacon's limbs felt useless. He couldn't move. He became aware of the sergeant on the desk eying him with suspicion. 'Can I help you, sir?' Deacon opened his mouth. He couldn't get words out. He struggled to his feet and lurched his way out of the front door. All he could think was to get away. Why hadn't the man said he was police? Why hadn't he taken details? What had happened to the injured man? Nothing on the news? So many things didn't seem right. He needed to talk to Mary.

He had a sickening sense their cover had been blown.

He entered the cabin, trying not to wake the children, felt his way in the dark to his and Mary's bedroom, whispered, 'Are you awake? Mary ...'

He fumbled towards the bed, so damned dark, leant over to shake her but his hands met only empty bedclothes. He recoiled. He tiptoed to the bedroom the children shared, eased open their door. On that side of the cabin the moon filtered its light through the curtains onto the beds, enough to show they were empty. His blood froze. He backed into the corridor, stumbled through to the bathroom, the living room to the balcony, confirming the whole cabin was empty. He had the only vehicle, so where the hell could they have gone?

The mobile phone rang with the impact of a gunshot. Deacon grabbed it and sank to his haunches against the wall. His heart slammed in his chest. He looked at the screen. 'Unknown caller'. He fumbled for the green button, then croaked, 'Yes?'

A deep, raspy voice answered. Craddock's. A fist squeezed the pit of Deacon's stomach.

'Did you think I wouldn't find you? After you killed my Paul?' A voice empty of emotion. 'Now I have your son, your wife and your daughter.'

'It was a bloody accident!'

A feeling of helpless rage drove Deacon to his feet. 'My family has nothing to do with this. If you want a fucking sacrifice for nothing, take me.'

'Nothing! My son is nothing? You murdering fuck. You were going too fast and you killed him. You're going to pay.'

The phone went dead. Deacon stared at it. He didn't know what to do, where to turn. Craddock had tentacles everywhere. The local cops had to be in on it. He and Mary had thought they were safe. What a joke. Deacon forced his mind to slow down. Somehow he had to find Craddock and get his family back. The detective who'd arranged the cabin, got them out of harm's way, Shandon, he had his number. But could he trust him? He'd done his damn best to get them away and keep it quiet and they'd had six months before Craddock found them. He had to chance it. He brought up and rang Shandon's number.

A groggy voice: 'Who, who's this?'

Deacon winced, looked at his watch: 2:30 in the morning.

'I'm so sorry. Is that Mrs Shandon? My name is Tom Deacon. I need to speak to Ray. He helped us a few months ago. We're in big trouble.'

'Yes, this is Adele Shandon. My husband spoke about you, Mr Deacon.'

There was a pause.

'You haven't heard. Ray was shot dead a month ago. They haven't found who did it yet.'

Deacon's energy drained away. His limbs went floppy and weak.

'Are you there, Mr Deacon?'

Finally he found his voice. 'I am so sorry, Mrs Shandon. I ... I ... oh God.'

He had no doubt Craddock was responsible. Craddock and his cronies. Too powerful, no mercy, not to be reasoned with. He was on his own and the bastard had his family. He had to do something. He forced himself to think. He had to get out of the cabin. It wouldn't take them long to come looking for him. He stuffed some food, water and spare clothes into a backpack.

Where to start? That guy with the severed arm had to be in the hospital. He'd see what he could get out of him.

He shoved the pack into his SUV and was about to climb into the driver's seat when he heard the sound of engines away on the other side of the forest and saw a flicker of lights through the trees. No time to waste. His daily runs had shown him a hidden track through the forest on the other side of the cabin. He left his lights off, had enough moonlight to steer by and spot the heavy burst of foliage screening the track. He eased the SUV through and puffed with relief when the foliage sprang back to cover his escape route. He flicked a small torch on briefly to see where to go and made slow but steady progress with the cabin between him and the other vehicles coming up the hill. He heard them getting closer but the crest of the hill was near. Once over he could switch his lights on and speed up.

When he hit the main road he sped towards the town. The streets seemed deserted, a ghost town, even the pub dead and dark. The hospital was about half a kilometre on the west side of the town. They'd been there once when Jason sprained his ankle. He spied a smattering of lights in the distance. A well-lit entrance with several cars parked in front. Otherwise quiet, no people about. He switched off the lights and glided to a stop in a dark patch a hundred metres short of the hospital.

Using the dark as cover he approached on foot. Through the main doors he could see a nurse, with her head down, behind a large, semicircular desk. He angled around the parking lot, keeping out of her eye line.

Concealed behind one of the cars he saw an intermittent flash of coloured lights, about a half kilometre away. An ambulance, no siren. That meant there were patients aboard. His stomach lurched, wondering if it was Mary or the children. He waited, his hands gripping the car's side mirror, almost tearing it off, while the ambulance swept into the emergency bay at the front of the hospital. Medics leapt from the cabin and ran to the back. With his eyes fixed on the back doors of the ambulance Deacon picked up in his side vision the arrival of a police car and another ambulance. The back doors of the first ambulance opened wide and the medics pulled a stretcher out. Deacon craned to see who was on it. He thought he recognised Craddock, his face covered by an oxygen mask, his limbs held down by straps.

The police car doors were flung open. The first out was the police officer who'd taken over at the forest. Seconds later the back doors of the second ambulance opened and Mary stepped out with jagged red-brown splashes down her front. Deacon could see she was close to losing it as she reached back to help the children down. They looked like they'd stepped out of a zombie movie. Pale, staring eyes, wooden movements. Deacon stifled a cry as he moved from behind the car and made to go forward. It happened fast. Three police officers with guns raised blocked his way.

'Down on your knees. Lift your hands high!'

Shock drove Deacon to obey, his hands flailing for the sky.

He heard Mary scream, 'No, don't shoot! That's Tom, my husband.'

The man from the forest stepped between them, raised his hands and called out, 'Guns down. I know this man.'

Before Deacon could speak, the officer introduced himself as Detective Chief Inspector Brian Johanson. He explained that Craddock had been critically injured but might survive. If he did it was likely he'd go to prison for a long time, if only for the kidnapping.

Deacon looked at him in disbelief. 'How's that going to help me and my family? He can still run his crime gang from jail and send his people after us. We're no better off.' Deacon felt fresh worms of dread wriggling. 'You used me and my family as bait. Craddock would never have got his hands dirty without a strong personal reason to get involved. We were set up.'

'Mr Deacon, you and your family were under surveillance the whole time. Craddock moved earlier than we thought. But we tracked him and got your family away without harm.'

'What do you mean, without harm? My wife's covered in blood, close to a breakdown and my kids look like something out of a horror story. I thought we were supposed to be under police protection, in a place Craddock couldn't know about?'

Johanson shuffled. 'I'm sorry. Senior Sergeant Shandon was snatched a few weeks ago and tortured before he was shot. We believe Craddock got your whereabouts out of him. We had an undercover officer tip us off. He's the one had his arm hacked off. Wasn't for you he'd have died. We're grateful ...'

Deacon went quiet, kept shaking his head.

'Unless Craddock dies, we'll be even worse off. He'll be more determined to get us.'

'We'll shift you again, maybe even out of the country.'

Deacon heard the words, thought how bleak their future sounded. He thought, too, that it could be a case of getting out of the forest, only to be back in the thickest part of the trees without a compass. A sense of hopelessness threatened to drain all his strength until he heard the big double doors of the hospital crash open. He swung round. Mary stood there, a huge smile lighting up her face.

'Craddock could die. I heard the doctor telling the guards.'

Deacon almost burst out laughing at the incongruity of celebrating a possible death in a hospital.

He called out, 'That's it, Mary. No more running or hiding. We'll take our chances. We're going home!'

Something No One Else Can See

Edwina Shaw

Red earth smells like my daddy when he's happy. Like he was before, when he used to sit beside me in the cane fields in his dirty work pants, put his arm around me and tell stories about when he was little like me and believed in fairies and magic dust. Mummy smelt like milk and canned peaches. I still smell her. I tell the others, but they don't believe me.

In the golden sun after school, I dig my fingers deep into the earth between the sugarcane that rustles and whispers above my head. 'Hush, hush,' the leaves say. 'Stay still, sit quiet.' Beads of sweat drip from my face and make dark splotches like tears in the red dirt as I dig. I snag a fingernail and it hurts, but I keep digging. I don't want to stop, not ever. I'm going to make a hole deep enough to hide in, to cover myself over. So I never have to go home again.

I lie on my tummy and use both hands to drag out earth in heavy clumps till my elbows are in, then all of my arms, and the front of my school uniform is covered in dirt. I scrape out the hole making it wide as well as deep, sliding my forearms up the sides, scooping till it's enormous, the biggest hole I've ever dug. Ever. Maybe the biggest in the world.

When I'm done, I lower myself in.

The hole isn't big enough. My knees are jutting out either side of my elbows and my top three buttons are out, as well as my head and muddy arms. I feel like crying. But then I remember to ask the fairies to help.

I help them, so it's only fair. Daddy used to say, 'You scratch my back and I'll scratch yours.' Then I'd scratch his back and he'd scratch mine and tickle me too, until I couldn't take it anymore and had to call out, 'No, Daddy! Stop!'

It's not really about itches though, it's about helping. That's what Mummy said.

Every afternoon I help the fairies by making tiny houses for them to sleep in – little holes in the dirt with grass for bedding and twigs for roofs, flower petals for decoration. I sprinkle crumbs of cake on leaf platters and fill gumnut cups with water for them to drink. Perhaps an army of fairies will come overnight and dig the hole deep enough for me, sprinkle it with glittering fairy dust and make everything alright again.

&

'Sam! Sammy! Sa-MAN-tha!'

Anna, my big sister, calls for me across the field. I don't answer, though. She only ever calls me Samantha when I'm in trouble. She finds me anyway, sitting in my hole, head tucked between my knees, hiding. I see her knobbly knees when I sneak a peek out half an eye.

I don't say a word. Hold my breath.

'I can see you, you know. I'm right here.' She pokes me with what feels like a stick, but I don't budge. 'You're so dirty! Your uniform! Mum would've skinned you alive!'

I keep my head down and swallow hard. 'Don't.' She knows that's not fair.

She rests a hand on my back, but she'll never say sorry.

I glare up at her. 'I'm not going home. Not ever. I'm staying here in my hole.' Then I remember it's not big enough and change my mind. 'I'll run away!'

Anna jumps up and claps her hands. 'Yeah! Run away!' She pulls me to my feet. 'Come on, let's find a good spot for you. Then later I'll sneak you food and stuff. It'll be super fun.' Ever since she turned ten, she's been saying super a lot. She's so excited I'm beginning to wonder if it's such a good idea. She doesn't usually like my games. We always have to play her games where she's the queen and I'm her servant. I wonder if she just wants to have my toys when I'm gone.

Hand in muddy hand we run to the end of the furrow, the cane stalks clattering behind us. 'Rush, rush,' they say, 'run further, run fast.' Once we hit the light of the tractor trail at the edge of the creek, we clamber down and along the riverbank in the shade, past where the old croc lives. We follow the dark river till we come to the flat place by the rapids where the giant fig tree lives and sun falls in sparkly splashes through its leaves. We drag branches and palm fronds through vine boobytraps and lay them across the tree roots that rise up like fairy-castle walls. It will be the best fairy house ever. Big enough for me.

'I'm never going home,' I tell Anna.

She nods as if she understands and maybe she does. I bet she's sick of making us toast and putting me to bed. We're almost out of Vegemite.

'Maybe you can stay here, too,' I say, wriggling over to make space. 'See? There's plenty of room.'

Every morning Anna's eyes are swollen from crying, but she's the big sister so she has to pretend that it's just a snotty nose. But I know. I know more than they think. And though I miss Mummy so much it's like part of my insides have gone forever, it's not because of her that I don't want to go home. Because I still hear Mummy whispering to me at night. I still smell her peaches and milk, and in my dreams, she still holds me and tells me everything will be alright. She hasn't really gone far. I wish they'd believe me.

I can't go home because of Daddy.

He's there, but he's not there anymore. He doesn't smell like him. He doesn't talk. He doesn't eat. And it hurts my tummy to see him all pale and ghostly without his red dirt. It's as if someone's emptied out his insides and filled him back up with something dark and heavy. The air he breathes smells black like poison, so I don't want to kiss him. But then I feel worse because I know he needs kissing more than anyone. Sometimes I sit on his lap and use my fingers to force the corners of his mouth up into a smile, but as soon as I let go, they droop back down again like melting plasticine.

It's been weeks since the funeral and all the visitors left. We're down to the last frozen casserole the church ladies made, and all the flowers have gone brown. Daddy doesn't go to bed at night or get up in the mornings. He just sits in his chair in the loungeroom staring at the wall. Staring at something no one else can see. Something scary and awful and very, very sad. He doesn't care that I'm going to be a sheep in the school play, or that Anna isn't winning spelling bees any more. He hasn't even noticed that other farmers are already harvesting. He hasn't smelt of earth for a long time. Not since Mummy first got sick and he came home smelling like hospital.

Sometimes Anna and I yell at him and try to drag him out of his chair, tugging his hands like he's a cow stuck in mud. But Daddy won't budge and when we let go, his arms fall back, limp and soggy. Something inside him is broken. Something so bad even kisses won't help. We don't know how to fix him. So Anna puts a casserole in the microwave or makes us toast, and we eat tea watching TV around Daddy and pretend that he's normal. But he's not. We're not.

The other night, when we were watching a show with guns we're never usually allowed to see, out of the corner of my eye I saw Mummy. Looking at us all. I tapped Anna to show her but she just got grouchy and made me go to bed.

Anna and I are down by the river finishing off our hideaway, decorating it with flowers and stones, when we hear it.

A crack like thunder.

Loud.

Close.

We look up, but there isn't a cloud in the sky.

And we run. We run and we run and we run.

As if our legs are horses, we race towards the house, too scared to breathe.

CRACK! CRACK! CRACK!

Fireworks go off inside the house. I smell them burning.

Anna and I hover at the door. Hearts beating loud into the quiet. I clutch her hand and we walk in together.

Daddy is standing in the middle of the loungeroom holding his rifle. His chair is tipped over on its side. He's looking up and when we follow his eyes we see the holes he's made in the roof, light falling through them in shafts of gold, speckled with smoke and dirt and bits of ceiling.

He drops his gun and looks at us, his face all weird and scrunched. He holds out his arms and Anna runs into them and then he starts laughing, or it could be crying, or both of them mixed together. He lifts his head and calls to me. Stretches out his hand, almost smiling.

But I stay where I am and stare as Daddy and Anna stand together in the streams of light. Dancing and alive with fairy dust.

Do You Put Your Hat on Your Elbow?

Dean MacAllister

The bell over the door rings as I push it open, leaving a greasy palm print on the glass. Outside the day is bright and warm, but inside the store it is cool and dimly lit. Despite this I keep my cap and sunglasses on, moving between the aisles, my head down with the determination of a shark.

Get in and get out.

Two high-school boys stand in the corner with car magazines, which they snap shut at my approach not before I get a glimpse of bare flesh hidden inside the pages. The boys wear uniforms, the collars of their jackets lined in a blue and green pinstripe, advertising the richness of their parents.

One of the boys nudges the other. I hear him say the word 'óvszer'. They must be Hungarian. His friend giggles, his high pitch grating on my nerves.

I open the fridge door and grab the beers that I came for. With my head down I make my way to the front, placing the six pack of Diekirch on the counter. The shop-attendant looks up, startled. He appraises me, a curious expression across his face.

'ID?' he asks.

I frown. He has to be joking. I'm twenty-eight years old. Despite being clean-shaven, there's no way that I look under sixteen.

Not wanting to make a scene, I take out my passport and slide it across. He opens it, holds it at face level, looking back and forth between me and my picture. The corner of his mouth raises slightly.

He recognises me. That's why he wanted to see my ID.

He slides the passport back to me and, after scanning the beers, lifts them into a plastic bag. He gestures towards a nearby rack.

'Gummi?' he asks.

The boys in the corner burst out laughing, which sets the attendant off, his shoulders shaking hard as he joins in.

I slap some euros onto the counter, grab my passport and the bag, and take off without waiting for my change. The bell chimes loudly as I slam the door behind me.

I storm down the street, vitriol pouring out onto the pavement.

Fucking smart-arses. Luxembourg? Luxembourg! Are you serious?

In Ireland the locals in pubs would try to force the word 'coiscín' into a sentence, gesturing towards me with their eyebrows, like I wouldn't notice.

It used to be that you had to achieve something huge to become famous. You had to be the first person to do something big. Dr. Jonas Salk was famous because he discovered the vaccine for Polio. Yuri Alekseyevich Gagarin shocked the world when he became the first man to journey into outer space. Stalin, Hitler, Mao, Leopold II and Pol Pot all became famous for killing a butt-load of people. Any way you looked at it, if you wanted fame you had to change the world.

Now, that idea is so last century.

The Icelandic kids would cough the word 'smokk' into their fists. Even their parents would chuckle.

Winding my arm back, I throw the plastic bag at a brick wall. The bottles shatter.

So much for having a quiet drink in my room!

These days you can become famous in two ways: doing something violent, or doing something stupid.

When I was on a slow boat travelling down the Amazon River, the crew used to whisper the word 'camisinha', which I later found out, despite sounding like the Spanish word 'camisita,' didn't mean small T-shirt.

I reach the hostel and push through a group of loud Britons blocking the doorway. I ignore their insults and walk up to the desk, asking for my key. The Asian man standing there, whom I haven't met before, stares at me with his mouth slightly open. 'Room 28,' I repeat.

'콘돔,' he says.

'Piss off!' I retort, walking around the desk and grabbing my key.

'Hey!' he yells, but I'm already climbing the stairs. Opening my door, I grab fistfuls of clothing and punch them into my backpack. My breathing is heavy now and it isn't just because of the stairs. I'm so angry that I feel dizzy, my vision blurring as tears fall onto the lenses of my sunglasses while I pack.

If you want people around the globe to recognise you, either:

A) do something incredibly violent, or
B) get caught on film with a stupid look on your face, doing something humiliating..

When I was a kid I had so many things I thought I might grow up to be: a fireman, a scientist, even a zookeeper … but a god-damn meme?!

We used to know inventors. Now we know Constipated-in-class-guy.

We used to know writers. Now we know Old-man-with-painful-grin.

We used to know explorers. Now we know Annoying-young-girl-that-wants-you-to-cash-her-ousside.

These faces have been burned into our minds. We celebrate idiocrasy, while remaining apathetic to greatness. Olympians, doctors in war zones, leaders in science. All go ignored. Name every person you know that's currently living in space. Even just one. I know, right? Neither can I. That's the problem! Yet you can name a musician who accidentally fell off a stage.

That's one small step.

I gather my toiletries and towel from the bathroom and force them into the front pocket of my lumpy, hastily-stuffed pack.

If she knew that what she did would affect me this much, would she still have done it? Was she really that heartless?

Taking out my wallet, I sum up in my head how much I owe the hostel. Fortunately, I've got the correct change, which I remove and shove into my back pocket. I have no desire to interact with the guy at the desk a second time. I give the room a quick scan and feel confident that I've packed everything, before heading downstairs.

The Korean man sees me and his eyes widen. He snatches up his phone, scrambling to unlock it. I pull out the euros from my back pocket and drop them onto the desk without breaking stride. I'm already out the door and down the street before he can film me.

I manage to flag down a taxi without having to wait.

'Findel Airport, please,' I say, sliding my bag across the back seat. The old driver simply nods and pulls away.

Have you ever heard of the Swiss Cheese Model? It's a bit cheesy (I hope you just winced), but it's the only way that I can excuse myself for what happened. Everyone has gaps in their knowledge. Every person on this planet, even the professors and geniuses, the world-wise and prodigious have a basic piece of information that they are unaware of. Something that they weren't taught or shown.

Anyway, the Swiss Cheese Model explains accidental causation. Imagine that you cut some slices off a block of Swiss cheese and then push them onto a skewer. Now imagine those slices are spinning on that skewer in different directions. Rarely, the holes in the cheese will line up. Now picture those holes being gaps in your knowledge. The amount of things you don't know will determine how many holes there are and how large they'll be. But, every now and then, you'll be put in a situation where you don't hold that vital piece of basic information you need to respond appropriately.

I've only ever slept with two girls – two long-term relationships that lasted for years. I'd assumed that I knew everything there was to know about girls, relationships and sex. I'd considered myself to be an experienced and capable lover.

That was before I met Maddy.

'Which way do you want me to go?' the taxi driver asks. I take off my sunglasses and rub my eyes.

'Whichever way is quickest.'

The Ukrainians would mouth the word 'презерватив.'

Did you know that roughly seven per cent of American adults believe that chocolate milk comes from brown cows? That's over sixteen million people! Did you also know that studies have shown twenty per cent of the US don't know that hamburgers are made from beef?

Have you ever seen a full-grown man drop his pants the whole way down at a urinal? Who's going to walk over and hold them up for him?

Maddy was a cute English girl who I met out one night. Her short, curly-blonde hair framed her face well and she was just as attractive out in the street light as she was in the treacherous lighting inside the bar. I had been nervous picking her up, as I'd never had a one-night stand before, but from the moment she first shouted her name over the loud music, I knew that I wanted to be with her. Short or long term, it didn't matter.

We'd made out in the taxi on the way to my place, and with our wandering hands it was obvious where the night was headed. Bursting into my apartment, we tried keeping our laughter down to avoid waking my neighbours. We collapsed on my bed and kissed passionately. She pushed away from me.

'You have any jimmys?' she asked.

'Sorry?'

'Condoms.'

'Uh, no. I've run out,' I lied.

Maddy rolled over, turned on the room light and began searching through her handbag. She stood up and threw a condom packet at me.

'You put this on and I'll freshen up, yeah?' She gave me a wink and grabbed her bag, going into the bathroom.

I removed my clothes as quick as I could. With all the foreplay I was ready to go. I tore open the packet and with a little fiddling managed to put the condom on. Ever since I'd broken up with my girlfriend, I'd been working out nearly every day at my local gym. I was more than comfortable with my naked body, so I lay back with my hands behind my head in a way that I thought looked seductive. Maddy only took a couple of minutes before she walked out of the bathroom in what looked like expensive black lingerie. She posed in the doorway for a moment, before walking slowly towards me.

That was when she had burst out laughing.

'What?' I asked, confused.

A strange look appeared on her face and then vanished. She smiled.

'Nothing, sorry. Now close your eyes and don't open them until I tell you, okay?'

I smiled and closed my eyes, eager to see her naked.

After about ten seconds I heard the sound of a camera going off. I opened my eyes to see that she had her dress back on with her phone in her hands. I frowned and I heard her camera go off a second time. Before I could cover myself, she had grabbed her bag and was out the front door.

I'd never been more confused in my whole life. I stared at my penis wondering what she was laughing at. My last two girlfriends had said it was a good size. One even said that it was big. Neither of them ever laughed at it before.

It wasn't until a month later I realised with horror what had happened.

A so-called-friend of mine tagged me on an online post. It turned out that Maddy was 'Instafamous,' with over 150k followers. Her profile was mostly semi-nude photos of herself, covering her nipples and private parts, with inspirational quotes like: 'You can achieve anything if you truly believe in yourself,' and 'To be a success you have to go further than everyone else around you,' which I took to mean that you had to show off as much of your body as the app would allow, before it deleted your page.

I opened up the post I was tagged in and there I was, au naturel, in two photos, one above the other. In the top photo I had my eyes closed, the other open. In both of them I had a dumb look on my face. Over my genitalia in the photos was a cartoon penis with a flat condom sitting on top of its head. Beneath the pictures she had described the night, explicitly. The description ended with multiple exclamation marks.

Scrolling through the thousands of comments below, my heart sank so low that I felt that I might need to crap it out. Nausea crept up inside me.

Let's get this straight: before that night I'd never worn a condom.

I'd never seen one put on in a classroom. Had never seen one put on in a porno. Had never taken the time out to read the side of a condom box. I'd always assumed that you just placed it on the top and when you inserted yourself it would roll on unassisted.

The holes in the cheese had all lined up.

In Nigeria the slang word for condom is 'okpuamu', which fittingly means 'penis hat.'

The taxi arrives at the airport and I find myself trying to buy a ticket for the next plane to South Africa. The lady behind the counter informs me that if I buy a one-way ticket, I'd need to organise a visa. I curse to myself and assure her that I'd organise on-going flights at the other end. She gives me a ticket for a flight that is about to board. I check in my luggage and run through the airport, filling out forms and scanning luggage, being reminded every time that my flight is about to take off. By the time I make it to my gate I'm the last person to board. The lady at the door smiles politely as she tears my ticket, but pauses before handing it back to me, giving that *where-do-I-know-you-from* look.

I snatch the ticket stub off her, jam it into my passport and hurry down the loading bridge to the plane. The steward asks for my ticket, as if I can't figure out how to read the seat numbers. Reluctantly I hand it over and he points in the direction where I already guessed my seat would be. I push along the aisle and see that everyone already has their seatbelts clasped. Some heads even shake as I shuffle along with my bag, staring at me as if being the last to board will somehow delay their flight.

I hear whispers as I make my way to the back of the plane, like voices in my head.

'Préservatif. Prezerwatywa. Bħala kontraċettiv,' whisper the French, Polish and Maltese voices.

I push on as if I can't hear them.

Finally making it to my seat, I stow my bag above me and am relieved to find that I have both aisle and window seats to myself. I take off my shoes and push them under the seat with my feet.

That night with Maddy was now five years ago and it may as well have been yesterday. The last word you want to hear after a night of intimacy is the word 'viral.' The pictures had been posted and reposted. Tweeted and re-tweeted. #Penishat had trended for so long that it was now seen as a retro-meme, resurfacing every time that someone publicly showed ignorance. Sometimes they would stick my dumb expression on celebrities' bodies. Other times people's heads would be stuck on my body, making them the temporary-idiot of the week.

Ever since I became a meme, I've been travelling from country to country, continent to continent, searching for people who wouldn't recognise me. Trying to hide somewhere exotic until the fallout blows over.

Picture Robinson Crusoe as a loser.

'Why don't you move to Antarctica?' one of my less-than-bright friends had suggested, not realising that there is no such thing as an Antarctican native. Not realising that the stations down there were full of people from around the globe who would recognise me as soon as I set foot on ice (as they did).

I could never return home either. Not after punching out Uncle Bob over the Christmas ham. I'd shaken his small, wrapped gift, instantly guessing what it contained. My small cousins had cried as he'd gone stumbling into the tree, crushing their presents underfoot and covering the rest of their gifts in blood and chipped teeth. The invitations to festivities had ceased after that.

Once, in Malaysia, I met this drunken Australian couple who told me about their honeymoon in Madagascar. They had taken over a *Madagascar* cartoon beach towel with them, thinking it would be hilarious. But they told me that the locals had never heard of the film, despite it being world-famous and based on their nation. That was the extent of the island's isolation.

So, that's where I'm headed.

From South Africa I'll fly to Mauritius, from there to Antananarivo, the capital of Madagascar. I'll head away from the French-speaking tourists and try to find a quiet spot in a coastal town, preferably one without Wi-Fi.

The Malagasy word for condom is 'fimailo.'

Hopefully, I'll never hear it directed at me.

At least not in jest.

Palm Reading, One Dollar

Joanne Anderton

The first catch of the day wears a pencil skirt and tall, black heels. Not the kind who usually stops to drop a dollar into my hat. Her palms are easy to read, a stark contrast to the mess of scars and tattoos across my own. They speak of long hours worked, doomed relationships, a nasty husband yet to come, and an ungrateful child who will never love its mother like she deserves.

In the past, I would have tried to warn her. I thought it was my job to arm people with the power to control their future. Now, I tailor my reply instead, and tell her only what she wants to hear. 'You are a hard worker,' I whisper. She has to lean forward to hear me over the voices and footsteps echoing through the tunnel. I know that means she can smell my unwashed skin, my unbrushed teeth, but I don't speak up. I draw her in. 'And you will get everything you work for. I see a husband in your future. I see a child.'

No one stops in this underpass because they want to hear a hard truth. Who pays a dollar for some great revelation?

I cannot look her in the eye, but I know she's nodding from the frantic bobbing of her straight, brown hair.

'Thank you,' she says, and pulls her hands out of my grip. 'Thank you.' She walks away.

I fold my own in my lap and hunch forward. What palm lines I once had are long gone. When I couldn't scratch them out I replaced them with new ones. Mandalas and symbols, heavy with meaning, anything to drown out the story imprinted there.

The crowd of weekday commuters surge past me in a never-ending flood. Another busker plays a soulful violin at the far end of the tunnel. I don't call out, I don't do anything to get attention beyond my small cardboard sign, written in thin texta: *Palm reading, one dollar.* Those who are destined to stop will stop, nothing I do can change that. You cannot escape your fate.

The next shoes that stop are solid black oxfords polished to a shine. 'You don't look like a fortune teller.'

I look up. Young, handsome in a rough-edged way, despite his tailored grey suit and sunglasses worn inside.

'You prefer your fortune tellers silver-haired and exotic,' I say, and it's not a question. No one really expects a fortune teller who is young and homeless, dressed in dirty jeans and a hand-me-down heavy metal shirt. They cannot imagine her only child in the custody of the state, at least until she can hold down a proper job. But that's harder than it sounds when she can't help but read the lines on her co-workers' palms. She's learned to lie about what she sees there, or at least keep her mouth shut, so that next time she's given the chance she won't get herself fired. Isn't that something? If she could just get a shower, and a bite to eat, and not spend her dollars at the bottle-o on the corner then she'd be back on the right track.

Sounds easy, right? But I know what her future holds.

He crouches then. I knew he would. Not because of my sixth sense, but because he wouldn't have stopped if he wasn't interested.

'Actually, you look like you could do with a good meal.'

There is a neat line ironed down the front of his trousers – it spreads across his knee when he kneels. He leans closer and peers into my face, removing his sunglasses. It forces me to look into his tired, brown eyes. A tiny teardrop has been tattooed beside his left eye. 'And where did you get those bruises?'

I hold out my ruined palms to him. 'One dollar,' I breathe, hoping he doesn't see the wreck of teeth in my poorly-cared-for mouth.

He digs for change in his pocket and drops a dollar in my hat. The chime of coin on coin echoes like a bell.

He places his right hand across my darkened palms. 'It's beautiful work,' he says. 'Your ink. I like seeing unusual work like that.' He pulls up his right sleeve as far as it will go. It's awkward, and the jacket doesn't move far, but it's enough to see the tail of some kind of dragon peeking out across his forearm. 'What do they mean?'

I shake my head. We're not here to talk about me.

I peer over his palm. His life reveals itself. The future and the past are connected; you can't see one without the other. So I read the struggles that brought him to this place. The abusive father, the absent mother, and the wrong crowd he fell so comfortably into.

'Listen to me,' he says, which annoys me. They don't usually talk while I'm reading. It's like he doesn't care what I see there at all. 'I can get you some help. Trust me, I know what you're going through. I know what it takes to change.'

I can see that he does. The contours of his past are filled with violence, with a madness I take to mean alcohol, drugs. Hard lines cut like wounds; rough lines caked with the dirt of the streets.

'Seriously, don't worry about doing this now. The dollar's yours, just keep it. Take my hand, let me help you—'

He tries to stand, so I grab his wrist to stop him moving. I see him hit rock bottom, and finally bounce. I see the shitty jobs he did to pay his way through college. I see the life he has made helping people going through the same things he has. I see a girlfriend he loves very much.

And I see the baby she doesn't yet know exists.

A little boy who will never meet his father.

'You've lived a hard life,' I whisper. He's already so close, I don't need to draw him in. 'And dragged yourself out of the darkness. You help other people into the light. You have become a good man. And now, you want to help me.'

A tiny frown crosses his face, like he's wondering how I could know all that, then dismissing the thought instantly. Any second-rate charlatan could spout vague predictions based on his actions and tattoos.

Do I tell him this is a pointless way to waste his final moments on this earth? Do I tell him about a lifeline cut short, so short, an end so close I can almost see it, hear it, taste it?

'Come on,' he says, 'let's get you up.'

He pulls me to my feet. He tries to lead me to the end of the tunnel and out into the real world, and for a moment, I let him. One small step, a second, even as far as a third. And with each step I allow myself to hope that maybe I misread his palm or maybe, if I just go with him, I can alter the direction of his line.

But hope's a dangerous thing. For me. For him. So I plant my feet and look down at the off-yellow tiles and refuse to move.

Because no one can change fate, and I have learned the hard way not to try.

You just end up hurting them. Over and over again. Until that's what your life looks like, a tally of pain across your hand. And finally, you realise you're doing more harm than good, that every piece of advice you give, every warning, does nothing to save them from their fate. If anything, you seal it. So you stop trying.

A minute more of pointless coaxing and he gives up, let's go. 'I'll come back for you,' he says.

I stand there and watch him push through the crowd. 'Wait—' I whisper, too softly to be heard. 'Don't— don't go that way. Just … wait.'

He's hurrying, probably thinks I'll be gone by the time he comes back. And he's not wrong; usually, I would be. Never stay too long in a place, never get too close to anyone. Right now I should be picking up my sign and packing up my takings and heading out the other way. But I can't stop watching him, the way he glances over his shoulder at me, not paying attention to where he's going. Heading straight for the road.

And I didn't warn him.

'Wait!' the word rips out of me, a scream I cannot control. It echoes harshly from the tiles. The soothing violin screeches dead. A mess of faces all turn in shock towards me. 'Stop!' My voice is rough; I'm not used to speaking above a whisper. 'The road. Be careful!'

Does he stop? He's lost in the crowd; I can't see. Did he look back when I screamed instead of looking at the road? Or did he slow down instead? When I hear the shriek of tyres I drop back to the floor and hug my knees. I press my face against my legs and try not to listen to the shouting, the sirens.

Where was he when the car hit? I didn't see that in his palm.

Routine

Mat Ward

Gerald Jenkins found himself staring at his feet on a normal Melbourne morning, gripped by the feeling that something unusual was happening. Much to his surprise he was pulling on the left shoe before the right one. He paused to think. He couldn't think of a time when he hadn't put his right shoe on first.

He'd woken up as usual, three minutes before the six-thirty alarm buzzed. He'd done his usual stretches and heard the usual creaking and clicking sounds from his forty-two-year-old body. He'd eaten his usual breakfast and ignored the usual talk show on the kitchen radio. He'd spent the usual fourteen minutes in the bathroom before getting dressed for work. He was thinking his usual thoughts about nothing in particular when the shoe surprise had broken his morning routine.

Gerald contemplated the shoes. They were a ridiculously pointy Italian make with a name he couldn't quite pronounce. The brightly clad girl in the shop on Chapel Street had insisted they were the right thing for him even though what he really wanted was something simple and comfortable. He'd never thought of this pair as *his* shoes. They were always just *the shoes*. If he put *the shoes* on, he'd probably go about his day as if nothing unusual had happened and he'd forget it ever had. He glared at *the shoes*. They were slightly too stiff and slightly too fashionable, but far too expensive for him to throw away. Now he had been given a sign and he'd be a fool to ignore it.

Gerald dug through the back of the wardrobe and found his old running shoes. These were most definitely *his* shoes, even though he hadn't worn them in years. He pulled them on, being careful to put the left one on before the right to keep the new rhythm going. He stood and took a few tentative steps. His feet felt like they'd come home to a warm embrace and he wondered where they were going to take him.

Gerald's feet took him as far as the coffee shop at his local train station before he realised he was falling back into the same old routine. The shop didn't sell the worst coffee in Melbourne, but only because they lacked the dedication required to be truly terrible instead of merely awful. He had a cup every morning.

Gerald decided to risk his train trip without a barely warm flat white to occupy his attention and give him something to grimace at. He ignored his usual standing spot near the rear end of the platform where he routinely waited. Instead, he walked towards the front, feeling a nervous tinge of trepidation as he looked around, trying to work out where the optimum spot to stand was in order to be perfectly placed when the train arrived. He couldn't see any obvious clues so he picked a central spot and stared across the tracks at a plain concrete wall with a dark green drain pipe dividing it roughly in half. He wondered what was involved in designing a drain pipe. Did architects specialise?

Gerald's thoughts were interrupted as the train arrived. All the good seats by the windows were already taken so he chose an aisle seat next to a young blonde girl wearing a beautiful deep blue Indian sari, opposite a bushy bearded man in a dark business suit. Both had paperback books in their laps and appeared to be completely unaware of their surroundings.

Gerald's usual commute survival technique involved blocking out the journey by plugging in his earphones and half listening to podcasts about celebrities he'd never meet and fabulous places he'd never go. Today he listened to the train and the people commuting with him. He listened to breathing and the train creaking and the wind rushing by outside and the occasional blast from the horn as they approached level crossings and stations. A faint *tish tish tish* from the earphones of the young man in jeans and a green t-shirt across the aisle from him. Screeching brakes. Coughs and muffled sneezes. Soft sighs. For the first time in a long time, he realised he wasn't alone. He was surrounded by people. All with their own lives.

Gerald had been told the best way to survive the world he'd found himself in was by following a routine. Get up, shave, shower, eat breakfast, go to work, attend meetings, eat lunch, write reports, come home, watch TV, eat dinner, go to bed. Wait for the weekend, go shopping, mow the grass, change sheets, take care of laundry, iron shirts, vacuum, dust, mop, clean. Keep doing the things that keep you alive, presentable and a member of the human race. Keep on keeping on.

He had asked what the point of it all was. There was never an answer that satisfied. Not seeing an alternative, he'd carried on with the act of following a routine, until he no longer thought about it at all. It was just what he did.

Gerald's train pulled up at his usual stop. He stayed seated, not wanting to let go of the sensation of connection he felt with the complete strangers who rode with him.

They passed through the Melbourne city loop, shedding passengers at each stop before reaching Flinders Street Station where finally Gerald felt compelled to leave. He could feel a buried knot starting to unclench deep inside him. It gave him a need to explore. A desperate ache to do anything that wasn't routine. He rode up the escalators to the wide, open concourse where commuters hurried in all directions. At the exit he crossed the street towards the uneven surface of Federation Square. He drifted towards a hole-in-the-wall coffee shop and studied the chalkboard menu. He considered the relative safety of a cappuccino but instead decided to be brave.

'What can I get ya?' the heavily pierced barista asked.

'What's a Melbourne Magic?' Gerald asked.

'It's like a double ristretto with milk.'

Gerald felt none the wiser. 'Ok, I'll have one of those, thanks.'

'Name?'

He hesitated. He'd always been Gerald, to his family, his friends and everyone who knew him. There was only one person who had called him something else. He needed to hear that name again. He told the barista, 'Gerry, with a G.' He handed over $10, pocketed the change and moved to the side to wait for his new coffee adventure to begin. He waited, switching his weight from one foot to the other, until his name was called. He approached the counter where he collected a takeaway cup with "Jerryg" scribbled on one side.

Peering under the lid, he saw what looked much like a flat white. He took a tentative sip. It didn't taste familiar. It was strong and powerful while still being smooth and easy to swallow. Gerry finally understood how people could become addicted to drinking this stuff, instead of grimly forcing it down every morning. He finished the cup and dropped it into a nearby bin, wide awake and ready to explore.

Gerry walked down a nearby flight of stairs, through a pair of automatic sliding doors which he remembered led to a large gallery of Australian art. He hadn't viewed any art in a long time. The abstract computer-generated prints on the walls in his office building didn't count. For the next hour Gerry drifted through the gallery. He stopped and gazed at everything he encountered, trying to understand the artist's intentions. The knot inside of him loosened further, encouraged by the many different ways people were able to express themselves. Portraits, landscapes, sculptures of all colours, shapes and styles. Eventually he came across an abstract statue carved from pink and white marble and walked around it, seeing different things at every angle. From one position it was two lovers entwined in a passionate embrace. From another it seemed to be a single figure silently pleading. Or it was a confusion of curves and angles forming vaguely despairing faces. A small placard declared the statue was named "Eternal Shadows of Love Long Lost". He felt unexpected tears as unbidden memories began to rise. He pushed them back down. He wasn't ready.

Gerry sat on a bench near the statue and wiped his eyes. He pulled a tissue from a pocket and delicately blew his nose. It had been over four years since he'd last cried.

A soft Irish accent interrupted his thoughts. 'Are you okay, love?'

A woman in a dark blue skirt and jacket was standing next to him. She had short brown hair, light blue eyes and a friendly smile. A nametag read Siobhan.

'Yes, thanks,' he replied. 'Just a little overcome, I guess.'

Siobhan nodded thoughtfully. 'Art has that effect on me too. Anything with horses, or dogs.'

'For me it appears to be abstract lumps of rock,' Gerry said.

'Sounds like my ex-husband.'

'He cried at sculpture?'

'No, he was an abstract lump. May as well have been made of rock.'

Gerry snorted and laughed.

'There you go, all smiles and snorts,' Siobhan said as her smile grew into a big grin.

'Yes, thank you. It's been a long time since I laughed like that.'

'Well, isn't that a shame? Everyone should snort out a laugh at least once a day. It does a body good.'

'I'm sure it does. If only you were around every day to help with that.'

Siobhan raised one delicate eyebrow. 'Well now, there's a thing to say. And you and I only just met.'

Gerry felt his cheeks and forehead grow warm. 'No, I mean …' He wasn't sure what he meant. 'I mean you're lovely and kind and I'm not used to being smiled at by pretty women and I'm babbling like a fool. I'm sorry.'

'It's okay, love. I like a fool who cries at art.' Siobhan tilted her head to one side briefly, then held out a hand. 'I'm Siobhan. Pleased to meet you.'

Gerry stood up and took her hand, which was

warm and firm. He gave it a quick shake then reluctantly let go. 'I'm Gerald … Gerry.'

'Well, Gerald Gerry, I need to get back to reception before they send security to track me down.'

Gerry watched Siobhan walk away. He was feeling emotions he hadn't felt in over four years. She was a complete stranger, but that wasn't too much of a problem, was it? Could he ask her out? She seemed to like him. But what if she was only being professionally friendly? What if she was fed up with random men coming on to her because she was doing her job? She probably hated it. She'd gather with her colleagues after work and laugh about all the sad, pathetic no hopers. No, best keep quiet. Don't make a fool of yourself, Gerry. No more than you already have.

Siobhan paused under a large archway and looked back at him. 'I'm here Sunday to Thursday from 8 till 4 every day. Don't be a stranger, Gerald Gerry.' She gave him an over-exaggerated wink and disappeared through the archway.

Gerry had fallen in love on three separate occasions.

The first was a hot flash of teenage love that burned itself out over three weeks. They were consumed utterly, until they discovered they had nothing to say to each other when their lips weren't otherwise occupied.

The second was with a strong, bright and fiercely independent woman he met at university. She played guitar atrociously, sang even worse and never let that stop her. She burned with passion and joy and a hungry need to understand how everybody's mind worked. They were together for a year and a half until she broke his heart saying, 'I don't know who I am when I'm with you.' He never did figure out what she meant.

The third was during his early thirties. Images of the day they met were seared into his heart. What she wore. How she walked. Her smile brightening every little thing around her. The way she leaned back and used her whole body when she laughed. The little crinkles around her eyes and the corners of her mouth. The strength in her long fingers when he impulsively reached for her hand as they walked through the night and she enthusiastically returned his grip. The taste and texture and warmth of her lips. The promises in her eyes.

They married a few years later. A few years after that she was gone.

Gerry left the gallery and roamed the city. At every junction he let fate decide which way he turned. If the crossing lights were green, he crossed the road. If they were red, he'd continue walking around the block. His path formed a haphazard zigzag as he followed the whims of chance and timing.

Gerry walked past convenience stores, pubs, sports shops, jewellery emporiums, and stores selling all manner of clothing from high fashion to hipster youth. He'd seen them all before but today the city was vibrant – alive in ways he hadn't experienced in years. He dawdled down graffiti-strewn alleys between towering office blocks, marvelling at how talented someone could be with a spray can. He saw a small sandwich shop where he bought a baguette stuffed with salami, cheese and lettuce. He munched on the baguette, enjoying the crusty texture and rich flavours. Exceptional compared to his usual sad sandwich. Routine had always taken him down the same paths through the same old habits. What did routine ever do other than keep him stuck in his life? It ensured he got up in the morning, went to work, came home, ate, and slept, but it didn't allow him to move on or truly feel alive.

Gerry decided it was time to say goodbye to routine. It was time to say goodbye to being stuck. It was time to finally say goodbye.

Gerry made his way to a number 64 tram which took him south out of the city. He sat in silent contemplation, paying no attention to the few people who rode quietly with him. *What am I doing? Is this what a breakdown feels like? It doesn't feel too bad. Should I be more worried about what I'm doing? Am I now worrying about not worrying enough?*

After a twenty-minute ride Gerry hopped off the tram and walked along a footpath to a set of ornate cemetery gates. *The shoes* always brought him to this cemetery every Sunday morning. He'd walk past statues of winged angels, crosses in many styles, polished white marble and pockmarked grey stone. He'd walk among monuments to opulence and death before reaching a small garden where he'd find a simple grave stone under a white rose bush. He'd stand for a few minutes wondering if he should say something. He'd had to push his feelings deep down and lock them away or he'd break. If he spoke, he risked his feelings coming out and he knew he wouldn't be able to handle that, so he remained awkwardly mute. Then he'd lay down the bouquet of fresh lilies and irises, and leave.

Today wasn't Sunday and Gerry didn't have a bouquet of flowers. He hesitated at the gates, hands clenching to hold something that wasn't there. Then he realised he had brought something. He finally had something to say.

Gerry followed the familiar path to the tidy little garden and stood in front of the white rose bush. The grave stone was smooth black marble with the name 'Sarah Jenkins' inscribed in white across the top and 'Beloved Wife' and 'Much Missed' slightly smaller below.

'Hello, Princess,' Gerry said. 'I'm sorry, I don't have any flowers today. It's Thursday and I wasn't expecting to be here. I've come because I need to say …'

His throat constricted and he choked down a painful spasm.

'I've come to say goodbye. I'm sorry it's taken me so long. Sorry I had nothing to say. You don't know how hard it was for me to keep going without you. Everything was upside down and inside out. The world tipped on its side and nothing made sense.'

Gerry took a few trembling breaths before continuing. 'I nearly did something stupid and final to try and stop the pain. They gave me pills which worked in a way, I guess. They took the pain away. And every other feeling.' Large hot tears fell onto Sarah's gravestone.

'I saw a grief counsellor. I saw a few. The last one helped me set up a routine. Something to keep me going every day. To keep me alive. Except I'm not. Life needs change, but there's none. No change, no growth, no improvement. Just routine. I'm not a person anymore, I'm a to-do list.' Gerry knew Sarah would have thought that funny and he felt a smile cross his lips.

'Something changed today. I don't know why. Fate? Randomness? Maybe it's just time to stop living the routine. To stop being routine.' Gerry turned away from the stone, rubbing one hand across his chest. The knot deep down loosened further. He sighed deeply and turned back.

'I met someone. I mean, I didn't really. Not "meet" meet. I just spoke with someone who seemed nice and who was interested in me in a small way. I thought about talking to her some more. I realised I could talk with another human being and get carried away by conversation and connection. I could ask her out on a date, get to know her, learn why she's so full of life.'

Gerry crouched down and focused on the ground in front of the gravestone.

'I thought about sharing my thoughts and feelings. I felt like I could have thoughts and feelings again. Even if it didn't work out with this particular woman, I wonder if maybe I could meet somebody incredible and caring and warm and vibrant and fall in love and live a long and happy life. Maybe I could live again.'

Gerry's tears fell heavier and he wiped his eyes.

'I've stayed trapped in routine far too long. That's enough. I'm not willing to do that anymore. I'm here to say goodbye. I should have said it years ago, but I … I couldn't. I couldn't let go. Now I have to. I need to.' He reached out for the grave stone and pushed himself up to a standing position, leaving one hand resting on the cool marble.

'Goodbye, my sweet princess. Every day, since we met, you brought flavour to my daylight moments and colour to my dreams. Every night I fall asleep thinking of you and wake with your name on my lips. I once promised there would never be a day when I didn't love you, and it's still true. It always will be. But now I truly need to let you go.'

Gerry walked away from the garden, wiping his eyes dry with the back of one hand. He left the cemetery, heading towards the scent of the ocean on the early afternoon air. Head held high, he enjoyed the warmth of the sun and the sounds of people bustling all around him. His mind was clear as he walked and the knot of grief had almost completely loosened. At the foreshore he stopped and gazed at the city, towers of chrome and glass in the distance. In years past he had loved Melbourne, walking through the streets, eating in the many cafes, and drinking at endless bars and watering holes. He'd always felt it was truly alive in ways that most cities could only dream of.

He turned away from Melbourne and walked across the soft sand to stand in front of the gentle rippling waves. This was the spot where Sarah had asked Gerry to marry her. He had been standing right here looking out over the bay when he'd heard her soft giggle. He'd turned and saw her down on one knee, wobbling slightly, holding a simple silver ring in one outstretched hand. He had burst into tears and said, 'Yes, oh my God. Yes!' before she even asked the question.

Gerry closed his eyes and licked the salty sea breeze from his lips while the sun warmed his back. He turned slowly in place, letting the cool breeze and warm sun envelop him. Allowing the memory of that day to fill him with the happiness that it held. Allowing his grief to wash over him.

Routine could keep him safe from pain and grief. He could take a step back to routine, back to safety, back to being numb, no risk, no feelings.

Or he could choose to be free and take a step forward to something new. There was the potential for joy and wonder, but also so much hurt. Could he step forward when he knew how much it could hurt?

There was a third option. He could step out

into the bay, keep going, and let the water take him away where he'd never again have to worry about heartbreak and loss.

At home, *the shoes* were waiting for him, ready to wrap him in their stiff but familiar embrace. In Gerry's past there was misery and grief. He didn't know what his future might bring. Maybe the grief would never leave. Maybe he could learn to live with it and balance it with new joy. Gerry knew there were events he could not control that could change his life completely. Simple things like randomly putting *the shoes* on in the wrong order, forcing him to see life from a different perspective. Or an intriguing encounter in an art gallery, stirring up unaccustomed thoughts and feelings. Or a driver reaching for a ringing phone and taking his eyes off the road for a split second, wiping away all meaning from the world.

Gerry opened his eyes and looked down at the reflected sky. Step back, step forward or step out? There was only one answer. Gerry knew what Sarah would do as he whispered, 'Goodbye,' took a step and felt the last ties of routine fall away.

The Salt Wife

Rhiannon Raphael

Every time we swim together my mother teaches me the same lesson.

'Hold tight to your coat,' she tells me. 'Every man who walks the earth will want to steal it from you, but you mustn't let them. Keep it wrapped close around you; that's the only way to stay safe.'

'Has a man ever stolen your coat, Mumma?' I ask, with the cruel ignorance of a child.

She is silent. Salt water swirls coldly around us.

Her lesson screams in my head when the net catches me.

It happens too fast to escape. I was focused on chasing a school of silver trout and didn't even see the boat. The school suddenly scattered and everywhere the water was laced with thin strands of silk. I tried to turn and swim away but the silk tangled and tightened painfully into my skin.

Now I am being dragged upwards, out of the water and into a small fishing boat. I struggle and thrash and try to get back to the sea, but it's no good. I am caught and above me looms the cold form of a fisherman and my mother's voice is in my head, screaming, screaming, screaming.

Hold tight to your coat.

The fisherman stomps one heavy booted foot down on the trailing end of the net, pinning it in place. He walks the net's length until he is beside me, trapping me with the weight of his body. I can't struggle anymore. The net is almost tight enough to slice through my coat.

Keep it wrapped close around you.

The fisherman pulls a short knife out of his boot. I shudder and consider shifting. Surely it is better to give my coat up freely than have it cut off my body?

That's the only way to stay safe.

'Be still now,' the fisherman says, and I am so shocked that I obey. That was not a man's voice. Now that I look more closely, I see the shape of a woman wrapped up in thick wool and heavy oilskin.

The fisherwoman places a steady hand on my coat and works the tip of her blade in under a few strands of the silk. She flicks her wrist upward and a section of the net slackens.

'I'll have you free in no time,' the fisherwoman says. Her voice is low, soft and soothing.

She is true to her word. A few more careful cuts and I am wriggling free of the net. The fisherwoman steps out of my way as I roll and shuffle awkwardly back into the sea's cold embrace.

Returned to the realm where I am free and weightless and strong, it is easy to follow the boat. The fisherwoman sails to a small cove, tucked away on a part of the island far from where the other humans live. When I lose sight of her, I leave the water, shift, and shrug my coat off. I can't wear it in this form, but I hold it tight against my chest.

My newly-formed legs tremble beneath me as they take my weight. The stones of the shore grind together loudly under my feet, making my trek up the beach wobbly and precarious. I've worn this form before, but never for long. It's useless in the water, and my mother's tales of the years she spent imprisoned on this island have kept me away. But now curiosity overrides caution and pulls me further inland. The human who caught me seems different from the ones my mother warned me about, and I need to know why she set me free.

The fisherwoman's home is a small cabin, freshly built against the rock walls of the cove. She is sitting outside next to a small fire, her ruined net draped across her lap. I approach slowly, trying not to be distracted by the unfamiliar sensation of my toes curling involuntarily with each step.

'Girlie, you are soaking wet,' the fisherwoman calls to me, 'and you've got no clothes on. Aren't you cold?'

'I have my coat,' I reply, holding it hard enough to squeeze water out from the layers of wet fur. 'That's all I need.'

'All the same, you're welcome to share my fire.'

I creep closer, but not too close. Not close enough to catch. Her fire is very warm.

'A seal got stuck in my net,' the fisherwoman tells me. She is holding a delicate bone needle in her hands, threading new silk into the broken pattern of the net.

'Men don't usually fish around this side of the island.'

'I don't want to fish with the men.'

'Have you no husband, fisherwoman?' I ask.

She shakes her head, gestures towards the deep blue spread out before us. 'I'm a salt wife,' she says. 'I'm married to the sea.'

My laughter is loud and sudden, the sound a harsh bark. The fisherwoman stares at me, but soon relaxes into a smile.

'Married to the sea!' I say. 'I like that. I'm married to the sea too.'

'I suppose that makes both of us salt wives then,' she says.

I laugh again and join her by the fire. The flames are small and sputtering, but it's the most heat I've ever felt, and it's enough to dry the water from my hair and leave a tangled mess in its wake. The salt wife watches me try to pull my fingers through it with some bemusement before sighing and setting aside her net and needle.

'I'd best fetch you a comb,' she says, rising and heading into her cabin.

'I'm sorry about your net,' I call after her.

'Don't fret about it, love. It's been torn before.'

When she returns to the fire she gestures to her feet. I settle there, with my back resting against her legs and my coat tucked into my lap. Her rough hands work the comb gently through the salt-stiff knots in my hair, and we talk into the night.

The first time I enter the salt wife's home, I touch nothing, and keep my hands tight around my coat the whole time. But inside is dry and so very warm, and the salt wife cooks me fish for dinner and hot toast with salt butter in the morning. Little by little, I relax my grip in her presence, and by the time she takes me into her bed my hands are in hers, and my coat falls forgotten to the floor.

When I wake hours later, the cabin is dark and the salt wife's warmth is missing from her bed. I am afraid. I crawl across the wooden floor, searching with increasingly frantic fingers. I find nothing, and choke down desperate sobs.

The front door to the cabin creaks open. The salt wife is there, silhouetted in the doorway. Returning from hiding my stolen coat somewhere I will never find it.

'What's wrong?' the salt wife says. She steps towards me. She is holding a lantern, and as she crosses the threshold the flickering light slides over her oilskin, hanging from a hook by the door. Next to it ... my coat!

I lunge to my feet and dash for the doorway, barrelling past the salt wife. She reels back and I grab my coat and wrap it around me even as I keep running. I don't stop when I hear her call out to me, don't stop when I am waist deep in the water and my coat is gathered around me. I shift and dive and swim away from the warm embrace of the salt wife, back into the cold and lonely sea.

She takes her boat out at sunrise. That's good. I have spent the pre-dawn hours swimming in small frustrated little circles beneath the waves, worrying that she won't want to see me again.

I wait impatiently for her to lower her nets. By now I know how to avoid the silk trap. But long minutes pass and no nets appear. Cautiously, I swim up until my head breaks the water.

The salt wife is there, but she is not fishing. She is waiting for me, watching the waves with eyes that are heavy from lack of sleep.

Still in the water, I shrug out of my coat and shift until I am wearing a form with two legs and a voice that the salt wife can understand. I climb into her boat and sit with my legs trailing in the water. She sits beside me.

'It's good to see you,' she says. 'You frightened me last night.'

When she turns to look at me, the sunlight catches in her curls and turns them golden. She usually weaves her hair into a big braid before leaving her bed, but this morning it is loose. She has been trying to teach me how to braid, so I know how soft those curls are. I want to bury my fingers in them now, and tug the salt wife close enough to kiss. But I can't. Not without letting go of my coat.

'I'm married to the sea,' I say. 'I can't stay away from her for too long.'

The salt wife nods. 'I don't want to keep you from your home.'

Instead of feeling reassured, her words leave me oddly … disappointed.

The next time I return to the salt wife's cabin, my hands are shaking. She greets me at the door with a kiss. I remove my coat and offer it to her.

'For you,' I say, shy but determined.

'Thank you,' she says. She takes my coat, and hangs it on a hook next to her oilskin.

I stare.

She steps away from the door, drawing me with her into the warm cabin kitchen.

'I made your favourite,' the salt wife says. I can smell fish in the air.

'Don't you love me?' I demand. My eyes are stinging.

The salt wife frowns, puts our plates down on the table, and wraps her arms around me. 'Why are you crying?'

'You're supposed to take my coat,' I say. 'If you keep it hidden from me, I'll be forced to stay here with you forever. We'll be married.'

'You want to be my prisoner?' the salt wife asks. 'What about the sea?'

'I love the sea,' I say. 'But she is not my wife any more than she is yours.'

The salt wife's arms are still around me. Her embrace is warm, but the words she whispers against my neck are cold.

'I've been in a marriage like that before. It's not what I want for you.'

She sounds like my mother when she says that, and I understand.

'But I still want to be yours,' I say.

'I thought you were already,' she says.

'I can't be. Not if I still have my coat.'

'Says who?'

'Says everyone. All my mothers and sisters and aunts and granddams. We either keep our coats on and stay in the sea, or we go ashore and are wed. That's how it's always been.'

'Well if I'm to have yours, then you best have mine.'

The salt wife takes her oilskin from the hook and wraps it around me. It smells like her, and I can't help but laugh.

'I can't take this from you,' I say. 'You'll freeze without it.'

'And you'll fare better, wandering around in your altogether?' she teases.

'You'll keep me warm.'

'But I won't keep you prisoner,' she says. 'I caught you once, and didn't much like it. I prefer to let you go, so you can return to me as you please. That's a better way to be married, by my reckoning.'

I frown. 'But who will keep my coat?'

'Why don't we share it?' she suggests. 'You wear it out in the water, and when you're home I'll keep it safe for you.'

'That sounds perfect,' I say, and kiss my salt wife.

Fallout Lives

Jessica Chapman

We had grown complacent waiting for Them to come. Maybe we were even beginning to believe They wouldn't. But then the boats were spotted and we were reminded that we were not an island completely forgotten. I took our dog, Duke, for a walk down in the reserve the morning after we heard. What else was there to do? How long would it take for them to invade this island? And I always took him for a walk on Saturdays. Down in the gully, aside from the walking tracks carved between the ghostly white gum trees, the landscape looked the same as it had for thousands of years, untouched by the rampant expansion of Sydney.

It hadn't changed in the years we had been waiting for Them to reach us. As Duke sprang through the undergrowth chasing unseen rabbits, I could almost forget that I wasn't still a flight attendant flying out to London the next day where Sophie would buy me a good curry and we would talk about everything, our worries disappearing as soon as we spoke them to each other, by the magic that only exists between sisters.

It was while walking back out of the gully that the truth was impossible to ignore. The first house I saw sat derelict with tufts of grass growing out of the cracks in the walls and roof. Two cockatoos were perched on the gables like antipodean gargoyles. One of them screeched, causing Duke to jump. Further up the hill the lawns had been dug up and replaced with vegetable gardens. The biggest difference, not the one you noticed right away but the one that made the suburb feel the most odd, was the absence of cars. This suburb had been built for cars with triple garages. Before, there were always at least a dozen parked cars in sight and now you couldn't even hear the noise of traffic. There were a lot of things from our old way of life we'd retained since we had been cut off, but without imported petrol the car couldn't be one of them. The eerie silence reminded me: *They were coming.*

The day before that, all thoughts of Them had been far from my mind. There was only my day at work and then Luc's birthday. Every year he cooked for just the two of us, Boeuf Bourguignon with the mushrooms we'd spent ages cultivating. It was what we did since we'd married. Well, not really married, not legally anyway. He liked to cook in the kitchen alone and I knew when I got home at seven that he would just be finished.

He'd taste his handiwork and say with a sigh, 'Tastes just like home. All this needs is a bottle of Bouchard Aine et fils Bourgogne to go with it.'

This year I was prepared. I knew there had to be a bottle left over from before and I had scoured the city for it. As he spoke the words, I pulled the bottle out of my bag and placed it on the bench triumphantly.

'*Bonne anniversaire!*'

His eyes lit up. 'How did you ever …?'

'I have my ways.'

'What on Earth did you trade …?' The smile from his face dropped. 'You didn't?'

'What glasses are best for drinking it?' I asked, turning to the cupboard.

'The big ones. Hazel, did you trade your sister's record player?'

I tried to shrug nonchalantly as I placed the glasses on the table. It was one of the things she'd left in her room for safekeeping until she moved back. It hadn't been easy to let go, but it was the only thing that I could trade for the bottle of French wine. 'It's been eight years. I don't think she'll miss it.'

He rested his hand on my waist sympathetically, *'Oh ma cherie, comment peux je vous remercier assez?'*

'You can thank me by enjoying your extra-special birthday dinner.'

It was a lovely night. We chatted as we ate and drank half the bottle when Dad burst in from next door.

'I'm sorry to interrupt but I thought you should know now. We just saw on the news. Boats have been spotted just north of Cape York. They're not from New Zealand.'

Luc grabbed my hand. The life we had made for ourselves was over. They were coming.

They had been coming for eight years, not that we knew what They were. There were never any photos of Them. Eventually, we pieced together from the initial frantic text posts from overseas and the very few survivors who docked here in their fishing boats and yachts that it had been an invasion. As our astronomers scoured the records, they were able to see what we had all missed. They had come from the sky and we waited for our turn knowing there was nothing we could do.

I was a flight attendant then, still living with Mum and Dad because I was so infrequently at home. I had been lucky not to be overseas that day. But I didn't feel lucky. I was on the helpdesk trying to keep everyone calm while I explained to the Australians that their long-planned holidays were indefinitely postponed and to the foreigners who no one knew when they might be able to go home. Televisions in the background showed frightening clips of amateur footage from overseas. People ran, buildings burned, the sounds of shots and explosions punctuating the background. In some live-streamed footage, the US Army deployed in a New York street, then something large and silvery floated towards the camera before the image went black.

My shift had been over long before we cleared the people away and I could go home. Exhausted, I walked through the nearly empty airport, my short black heels echoing in the cavernous space. I then heard sobbing. As I got closer I heard the familiarly friendly but calm voice of a flight attendant saying, 'I'm sorry, sir.'

I turned my head and saw her standing over a chair where a man in a suit sat, his shoulders hunched and shuddering. A television above them flashed images of a street that looked like to be somewhere in France. She shot me a silent call for help and I approached them.

She whispered to me, 'I don't think he speaks English and I don't speak a lick of French past *bonjour*. I'm usually on domestic service.' The stress that we were usually so good at hiding began to show.

'I probably speak enough to handle it. Why don't you head home?'

The relief flooded through her tired face and she left.

'Monsieur, puis-je vous aider?'

As he lifted his head his tear-filled eyes met mine. In short sentences, clipped by sobs, he told me about his wife and children that he would never see them again. He dropped his head and I sat next to him laying my hand on his shaking shoulder. I tried to comfort him with the French I usually used to apologise to passengers irritated with the snack selection. I let him cry until his sobs softened and asked if he had somewhere to stay that night.

He shook his head.

Normally, I would have suggested a hotel, but as I looked up to see a shot of Buckingham Palace on fire I knew that the situation wasn't normal. There was something in his outward display of grief, the same feeling I had knotted up tightly inside me, that made me reluctant to leave him. I asked if he'd like to stay with me and my parents for a couple of days.

He nodded and stood up grasping the handle of his suitcase with a trembling hand. He followed me to my car. I texted my mother to cook extra for dinner.

We drove silently, lurching back and forward in the peak-hour traffic that had since disappeared.

'*J'ai envie de pleurer toujours,*' he said suddenly.

'*Pardon?*'

He repeated himself but the limits of my French had been reached.

'*Je suis désolée … mon français* … isn't great.'

He smirked. 'In English then.'

'Did you say that you still envy the rain?'

'No, that's the word-by-word translation. It means I still feel like crying.'

'Oh. Sorry … So you do speak English after all.'

'I do. Maybe I should have tried to listen and talk to the other flight attendant. I feel a bit bad now. Honestly, it was like I didn't hear anything until you spoke in French. I guess grief should be expressed in one's own language.'

I nodded. 'Or not at all.'

Our lives completely changed. We lived in the shadow of not knowing when They would come for us. They didn't come the first month, when every website outside of Australia and New Zealand disappeared. They didn't come that year, as petrol and diesel were rationed to primary industries only, or the next year as more people moved into the city to be closer to the trains and those who stayed in the suburbs where we lived dug up their lawns to plant food, or even the year after when the government started an initiative to manufacture household appliances like refrigerators on home soil again. Or the next when we resumed trade with New Zealand. Or the one after that when we grew so used to living our lives that we almost forgot what they were like before.

During the seismic shift of our way of life, Luc was always downstairs at breakfast with a smile and a *bonjour*. Mum and Dad welcomed him into the house with ease. The invasion suited them. Dad already grew his own tomatoes and tinkered with anything that didn't work. Their thrift, which had been an oddity, was suddenly an asset.

Luc and I quickly became friends. He was only supposed to be in Sydney for a week on business when he had been stranded. He often spoke of his wife, son and daughter. I spoke about Sophie sometimes. We talked in a ragged mix of French and English. I asked him to speak as much French as he could, even if I had to ask what it meant. I said that it was because I wanted to improve mine but really, I wanted him to preserve that part of himself. I expected him to move into the city where a small French community was gathering but I was glad he didn't. He said he preferred the air and space of the suburbs. Every now and then he took the electric bus to the French area to talk to someone who was fluent in his tongue, and he'd take a basket of vegetables to swap for books in French.

It was three years before we became more. I had a new job by then, just three days a week doing some customer care for the state government. Our lives were beginning to feel less strange. One day as I came home from the office, stepping off the electric bus and onto cracked bitumen, I saw Luc walking to me with Duke on a leash. When we met, I stooped down to give Duke a pat and he lurched forward and knocked me over. I giggled as I stroked his head.

'He missed you today,' Luc said.

'Well, he's going to have to get used to me working again. He was used to it before when I was away for weeks at a time.'

'He's a dog; there was no *before* for him. There's only *now* when you're a dog.'

'*C'est vrai?*'

'It's true! He has no sense of permanence.'

'Well, then he might already be used to it.'

'If only we could be as quick to adapt as dogs.'

I looked up at Luc. 'I don't know; I got used to you being around the house pretty quickly.'

Luc chuckled. 'But Duke was used to me the second day I was here.'

I loved the way Duke's name sounded in his mouth, round and short, almost unfinished, strange and familiar all at once. He held out his hand to help me up. I took it. When I was on my feet, I found myself closer to him than I'd expected. He still held my hand tightly; he seemed to stare straight into me.

'Hazel, do you think it's time we lived as if there was no before?'

'We? What do you mean?' I thought I should step back, but he seemed to draw me closer so I stood still.

'I mean … I … *Je t'aime.*'

The impulse to kiss him took over.

We lived as if we were married after that. But we were very careful about kids. Neither of us wanted to bring a child into a world that could be invaded at any moment – although judging by how many toddlers I saw around, plenty of people weren't. I walked up the hill to where our two houses sat, the home I had grown up in and the one I had moved into with Luc. Our neighbours moved to Queensland to be closer to their family. Luc and I moved into their house and we pulled down the fence to make a larger backyard for Duke to run in. We'd wanted our own space by then. It was hard to believe that They were coming and would destroy all of it.

As I approached our front door, Mum popped out of their house. 'I thought I heard you. Hurry, Hazel! Come see the news.'

I hurried into the lounge room at Mum and Dad's where we kept our only working television. Duke followed me inside. Luc and Dad were transfixed by news.

Dad glanced at me, 'Hazel, the boats … it's not Them. It's survivors.'

I looked at the aerial shots of the boats; the decks were covered with people waving their arms.

'Don't shoot, we're human!' they cried.

'Sophie could be on one of those ships,' Mum said.

'Mum …'

'Who knows what happened? She could be alive.'

I didn't know what to say. It wasn't until Luc touched my hand that I realised it was shaking. I had never told anyone about the last time I spoke with Sophie. It was over video chat. She was in her flat in London, the tiny third-floor walk-up, sitting on the sofa bed I slept on when I stayed with her. She swung back for her lunch hour so we could talk before I went to bed. We were talking about booking to see something at the Globe the next time I visited. There was a noise, she turned to look out the window behind her.

'Hang on, Hazel, something's happening outside.' The window broke.

I'm still not sure what it was I glimpsed. Every time I've replayed it in my mind the image gets dimmer.

A skinny, vaguely armlike … thing reached in. She stood up. She tried to run. The prongs at the end caught her foot and she toppled onto the computer. Her distorted scream rung in my earphones as the screen went black. I spent the night ringing every London police number I could but no one answered. Mum found me slumped over the dining table when she got up the next morning. I couldn't bear to tell her what I saw. It was only when I arrived at work and found out that the international flights had been grounded that I knew for sure it wasn't a nightmare. It was a secret I'd carried too long to share; I knew she wouldn't be on one of the boats.

In the days that followed, reports of the boats docking flooded in and interviews with survivors were constantly broadcasted. Here, we weren't sure what had happened or why They invaded. The survivors had resisted the invasion tooth and nail. But They only wanted the resources of our planet, They hadn't wanted to wipe us out. So They made a deal: They would leave Australia and New Zealand as a human reserve if all the remaining survivors would consent to move there. The survivors were welcomed into our cities after some brief quarantine procedures. Lists were drawn up and anyone seeking information about a missing loved one could check at Town Hall. I tried to delay but couldn't.

Luc came in with me. There were people everywhere. You could tell who the survivors were – they were skinny and their eyes darted at every movement. We waited and waited in long queues. When it was our turn Sophie's name came out in a croak and I had to repeat myself. The dark-haired lady typed the name in and looked at me apologetically.

'She's not on the list, is she?'

She shook her head.

'And there's no other boats coming?'

'I'm sorry, ma'am.'

'Thank you for checking.'

I don't remember walking out of the hall. I just remember standing next to Luc on the street and sensing him tense up next to me.

'Luc!' I heard a woman call. She was thin and frail and a teenage girl stood by her side.

Martine! Claire!' he exclaimed, running to them. *'Et Pierre?'*

As the woman shook her head, tears fell from her eyes. They embraced, a family reunited, crying together, for the loss of Pierre, for all the lost years. He'd told me so much it was almost like I knew her. I knew how much she meant to him, how hard it had been for him to lose her. And now she was in front of me and I wished her gone. The flash of envy left me sick. And what did his wife being alive make me? We had been together for five years, but was that worth more to Luc than the twelve he'd spent with Martine before that? I had to do what was right. It felt like five minutes before Luc turned back to me.

'They should come home with you,' I said. 'We have enough to feed them.'

The trip home was the longest I had ever been on. I should have told Mum and Dad on that morning eight years ago. I should have called in sick to work and we could have grieved Sophie together. Someone else at work could have found Luc a hotel room. I don't remember what I said, what variation of 'She's gone' I uttered to dash the looks of hope on my parents faces. I just remembered Mum throwing her arms around me and sobbing into my shoulder before she noticed the two women standing behind Luc.

She wiped away her tears. For her, crying could always wait until there was no more to do. 'But who's this?'

'This is Luc's wife and daughter.' I said, feeling like my whole body was empty.

She gave me a barely perceptible look of sympathy before she turned to them.

'Well, *bonjour*, welcome. Come in, make yourselves comfortable. You look hungry, I'll get dinner on.'

They both looked blankly at Luc. He spoke to them softly in French before turning back to Mum. 'Sorry, they've forgotten most of their English.'

'Well, let them know they're welcome to anything they want.'

Under the pretence of making up a bed for Claire, I went next door and put my clothes in a suitcase. I thought it would be hard to fit it all in but clearly I hadn't quite unlearned the flight-attendant habit of only living with what could be quickly packed up and wheeled away. It was surprisingly easy to remove all traces of me from the room. Let Luc decide what he told her about me.

Dinner was quiet and awkward and when it was over Martine and Claire said that they were tired. Luc and I took them over to what was no longer our house. I showed Claire the spare room and then Martine into the master.

Luc looked around the room with a look of confusion.

I held the bottles out to her. *Je vous ai apporté le shampooing et apres-shampooing.'*

Martine took them as if I were handing her a baby bird. *'Shampooing? Et savon?'*

I told her there should already be soap in the shower.

Martine grabbed my hand and squeezed it with such gratitude. *'Merci beaucoup.'*

'De rien,' I replied. *It's nothing.* Those two short words were never harder to mean. *'Bonne nuit.'*

It wasn't until I was downstairs that I realised Luc was following me.

'You moved your things out.'

'Yes, I'll go back to my room next door.'

He spat French at me so quickly I couldn't make out what he was saying.

'You know I can't understand when you speak it that quickly,' I interrupted.

He paused and drew a deep breath. 'You moved all your stuff out. Just like that. I can't believe how cold you are.'

'What do you want me to do? She's your wife. Your wife who has been through God knows what. And you want me to ... *what?* Demand that you're mine now and that you should tell her your marriage is over?'

'I want to know if the last eight years meant anything to you.'

'Luc, in the last eight years you have been about the only thing that has meant anything to me. If it weren't for you, I don't know how I would have survived. And I don't know how to keep going without you.'

Luc's shoulders dropped and he looked away.

'Does that help? Does that help you?' I realised I was almost yelling. He hadn't meant to hurt me, he just hadn't thought through the implications for me of Martine being alive. I stopped and pressed my temples. 'Does it change what we're going to do?'

Luc couldn't meet my gaze. I could tell he was struggling under the weight of decision. But I knew him well enough to know what he would decide. 'Hazel … I think you saved my life eight years ago but …'

'*C'est ta femme,*' I said.

'*Oui*. She's my wife.'

We stood for a moment, feeling the gulf between us widen, neither of us sure which language to say goodbye in. The clunky English goodbye felt too hard to say, but the French 'Till I next see you' seemed even more false. A last meeting of our eyes and I turned and left what was our house. A wordless end.

I returned to my parents' house. Mum was wiping down the kitchen, a nightly ritual that hadn't changed since before the invasion.

'Are you alright, honey?' she asked.

'No. I didn't even think that he might want to check if they were there, his wife, his *children*. It didn't even occur to me. I was too preoccupied thinking about Sophie.'

'Honey, he gave up on them long before you gave up on her.'

'I wish I'd been in London with Soph …' Sobs chocked out the end of her name.

Mum pulled me into her arms and held me like I was still a child, unselfishly holding back her grief to comfort me. 'I know you feel that way right now but you'll be okay in time.'

Time. It's been sliding past me since then; I've been dislocated from it. The people of Sydney welcomed the survivors with unprecedented warmth, understanding there was no home for anyone to go back to. We shared our resources and built our lives together. Everything was done with the knowledge that They could decide to take Australia from all of us at any time, a Them frightening enough to unite us humans.

Luc eventually moved into the French Quarter with his family. That was for the best. The house next door has been empty since. We still use the garden to grow vegetables. I wake up every day and do what I can, what I must to live. I still walk Duke every Saturday morning, even when it rains.

J'ai envie de pleurer toujours.

I still envy the rain.

David's Fish

Fran Collings

At night, David dreamt of the fish. He could almost touch the slippery scales, smell its fresh sea-scent. One night he stared into its eyes – cold blue-black discs. Always he awoke before he could land it.

Each day, as he tended his garden, or worked as a guide, David thought of his fish. It would be the biggest Spanish mackerel the villagers had ever seen. Its scales would shine silver, iridescent beneath the sun, the blue-grey fan of its dorsal fin erect and spiny. The fish would be long, its snout reaching the length of his humble outrigger.

As he worked, David wondered if the Australian would keep his word. He had shown Len around the island a few months ago. Len was one of many passengers from the great white cruise ship moored close to Kitava Island, off the coast of Papua New Guinea. David had approached him. 'Sir, I am official guide. Maybe you like tour of my island?'

Len had agreed and so David had shown him the village, taken him to the orchid garden and guided him to Skull Cave. David had fallen silent as they reached the cave. Deep within its recess lay the bones of his grandmother. They rested on a stone ledge, gleaming bleached white in the shadows. The long femurs, the notched spine and the polished skull had not yet yellowed with age. Grandmother had passed barely two years ago.

David had stood, head bowed. He was sorry this was not the real Skull Cave, the one shown on the signpost. That cave held the bones of many ancestors – some yellow, some new-white. But had Len followed the sign, he would have had to pay the guardian of that cave more money. Better David show Len the orchid garden he alone had cleared, and visit the cave of his own grandmother. David did not think she would mind. The money earned was for their family. It would help send her great-grandchildren to school.

As they left the cave, Len had turned to David. 'Saw some of your people smoking fish over a fire, as I walked along the beach.'

David nodded. 'Yes, often they do that.'

'I suppose you like to fish?'

'Yes, I like to fish, but unfortunately it not possible.'

'Why not?'

'Fishing line and hooks – I cannot buy them.'

'This fishing gear, you mean it costs too much?'

'Yes, sixty kina or more to get here. Thirty dollars Australian.'

'Reckon I could send you a spool or two, and some hooks.' Len had smiled. 'Heavy line.'

'That very kind of you. Fishing line would be wonderful thing.'

'Well, where should I send it? I mean, you must have an address.'

And so it had been arranged. Four months had passed and David scanned each supply delivery. He always returned empty-handed.

In late September, when fat grey rain clouds hung overhead, threatening an early monsoon season, the package arrived. The skipper of the supply boat handed it over, damp and dog-eared but intact. David fingered the wide, waterproof tape encircling the parcel. He walked back along the beach, squatted beneath a she-oak and slit the tape with his bush knife. His friends crowded close. The spools of thick sea-green nylon drew admiring nods. The packets of gleaming hooks and pupa-like brass swivels were passed around. David would finally be able to fish.

At the approach of the wet season, fewer cruise liners came. The yam festival was past and monsoon time drew near. In these quieter months, David carved sea creatures to sell when the tourists returned. He especially loved to create stingrays, with tilted wing tips and curving tails. But David could not settle to his carving or gardening.

'Today I will try for this fish,' he said to Manu, his wife. 'I must go before the weather turns bad.'

David clasped her hands within his own, then walked down the track from the village. He wore a faded red t-shirt, with many holes – his lucky shirt. In his *bilum*, a hand-woven string bag, he carried his fishing gear and water sloshing in a cast-off plastic bottle. His rusty gaff was slung over one shoulder. He turned, once, and waved as he saw Manu still standing at the top of the hill.

David dragged his small outrigger into the grey-green water and paddled past the sea-arm of the island. He must get through the break in the reef, the boat passage, into the deeper water beyond.

Today the tide was slack, so the pull was not great. David paddled his craft through the gap and into the main channel. Here the sea was inky, swift-flowing and deep. David let the outrigger drift as he threaded his heaviest line with a double hook and two silver bait fish. He tied the spool to an outrigger post and slid the line between his fingers, letting it spiral deep into the dark sea. He commenced paddling, gently, just enough to keep his course. He began a rhythmic pull and release of the line. His arms would grow tired by the end of the day but surely he would have a fine fish to show for his pain.

Time passed. The sun beamed hot as David sipped from his bottle. His line remained slack.

'Are there any fish at all in this channel?' David muttered as he pulled in his line. He checked his bait and hooks but nothing had been touched. He cast, trolled again. It was lonely so far out. There were no other boats in sight, or other signs of life. No birds overhead meant no fish below. David changed course, facing chop as he veered out to sea, further than he had ventured before. A fresh wind began to build, ruffling the surface.

David scanned the sky, still pale blue, with clouds gathering in the west. To his right he spied a squabble of sea-birds, gannets and terns: their shrill squawks and flapping wings drew David to them. He paddled, keeping one eye on the birds, the other on the horizon. He trolled again, his sinewy arms falling into the rhythm of pull and release.

It came swiftly: the urgent knock-tug on the line. David jerked back – he could feel the fish's panic in its sideways pull. The line shrieked off the reel, nylon scorching his calloused fingers. David let the fish run until he judged enough had streamed out. He pulled back, steadily reclaiming lost line. He stopped when the nylon was taut, when beads of water danced.

The sea gleamed glassy green as the cloud-mountains turned to grey. David could no longer see his line suspended below. The sky darkened quickly, with purple bruises of clouds swelling out to sea. An early wet season squall was brewing. He had just enough time to head back to the island before the storm hit. His outrigger was sturdy but he would be busy paddling and bailing water with his *yatura*, his wooden scoop, without bothering with the fish. He sensed this fish was a pig-headed one. One that would cause him much trouble. Already it was dragging the outrigger with its run.

He should cut the line, he knew. But he felt a connection between himself and the fish. He could not let it go. David pulled again. Far below, he felt the fish dance in a frenzy, zig-zagging back and forth. He released line once more, then – stillness.

The sea became sullen, stirred up – the chopping waves bounced beneath the outrigger. The first, heavy raindrops fell as David pulled and gained line. It coiled in sea-wet circles beside his feet. He felt only heavy drag, with no response. Maybe the fish was waiting, biding its time. Perhaps it was tiring. Who could tell what was in the mind of this fish, so many metres below? The rain set in, sheeting down. Maybe the fish could sense the rain, feel the turbulence as the waves sprouted waist-high around the outrigger.

The outrigger dipped steeply as water sloshed around his ankles. David used his free hand to bail with his old *yatura* before the craft became sea-laden. He hauled in line again. The fish fought back. Maybe, soon, it would begin to tire? David sensed it was a male, young and strong. Perhaps he would tire before the fish, after all. He was trapped in a relentless routine. He would give the fish slack, the fish would run with it. David would reclaim line, bail water, and the fish would streak the line out again.

The fish circled, diving beneath the outrigger. If the water had remained clear, David could have seen the long torpedo shape below the surface. All he saw was a shadow as it passed below. Waves reared shoulder-high and David knew a bigger swell would come as the wind swung full to the west. The sky was closing in, the horizon near. His world had become the sea, his outrigger and this fish.

The tugs came closer together, almost wresting the line from his hand, cutting it sharp and deep. Bright blood, scarlet as betel nut juice, dripped onto the hull of the outrigger and David bound the wound with a piece of torn *lap-lap* cloth. He did not want his blood to awaken the thirst of any shark.

The fish made another pass. David gave some line. 'Run, fish. Run with it. Tire yourself out.'

The power of this run took David by surprise. He spread his legs to brace himself. He swayed over the churning sea, managing to grasp the mast as he stumbled. The outrigger rocked, and dipped closer to the water. A wave broke, flooding the hull.

He bailed, then struggled to grasp the line with one hand as the fish bucked and strained. David reeled him closer, the line taut. Blood seeped through the makeshift bandage, dripping dark into the water.

The fish was close to the side of the outrigger and David grasped his gaff. He saw the Spanish mackerel shining silver beneath the waves. It rolled on its side, slashing the water with its deep-finned tail. Its belly was almost white. One eye swivelled, looked directly at David. Cold, black-rimmed.

It knows, he thought. *He is clever, this one.*

Thunder crackled and rain pelted, sharp as a shower of stones. David hooked the fish with the gaff. He could see the blue-grey bars running the length of its body as he dragged the fish half into the hull before bailing again.

It flexed its steel blue tail and sprawled, mouth agape, with curved needle teeth ready to slice a finger or foot. David hauled the rest of the fish into the boat, its gills gasping, gusting as he clubbed it. He feared it would overbalance the outrigger. It lay, twitching, along the hull. David threaded vine rope through its gills, and trussed it to an outrigger pole.

Lightning slit the sky, spearing fiery purple arrows into the ashen, white-crested sea. He gripped the paddle and willed the outrigger across the waves. Any one of those lightning spears could strike his boat, but he could not think that. Instead he prayed to the God he had learned of in mission school and fought his way back to the channel, stroke by stroke. His shoulders ached and pain seared the length of his spine. His throat was dry, choking. He longed to drink but could only open his mouth to catch the rain. The muscles of his arms were roped as liana vines, and his eyeballs bulged, red-veined and white, as he battled to the edge of the reef.

The gap was hidden beneath black, writhing snakes of water. Any of the foaming eddies could hide a coral *bommie*, wrecking his outrigger instantly. Once, twice, David made a run for it, then veered away as the narrow passage was lost in the boiling foam.

A crow-black wave banked behind him. David took his chance and went with it, riding its winged crest. It carried the outrigger high over the entrance. He surfed down into the churning waters of the bay.

Author Bios

Joanne Anderton writes speculative fiction for anyone who likes their worlds a little different. Her publications include the novels *Debris*, *Suited* and *Guardian*, and the short story collection *The Bone Chime Song and Other Stories*. She has won the Australian Shadows Award, the Ditmar and multiple Aurealis awards. Her most recent book is the children's picture book, *The Flying Optometrist*, and a complete departure from her usual genre. She has just completed a Masters of Arts in Creative Writing at UTS. You can find her online here: http://joanneanderton.com

Pamela Baker has had stories published in magazines like *Australian Short Stories, Idiom, Hecate,* and in the anthology, *Hidden Desires,* published by Ginninderra Press in 2006. She has won prizes and been highly commended in many short story competitions, including Boroondara and Alan Marshall.

Jessica Chapman is a Sydney-based writer with a Masters in Creative Writing. A world traveller since she was five-days-old, Jessica spent five years living in Pakistan as a child. Add to the mix a bizarrely harmonious relationship with her incredibly supportive family, an unparalleled ability to get food on her face and a pet Labrador who believes everything can be a chew toy. She is currently working on her first novel.

Fran Collings is a retired music teacher and her Mallee childhood is reflected in much of her writing. She has won several short story competitions including the Joseph Furphy Commemorative Literary Prize 2015, Society of Women Writers NSW National Writing Competition 2017 and equal first prize Society of Women Writers WA 2018, as well as second prize with the Henry Lawson Memorial and Literary Society 2019. She has been shortlisted for the Rachel Funari Prize for Fiction, Port Fairy ex-libris competition, Joseph Furphy Commemorative Literary Prize 2016/17. She has been published in

Imagine Maroondah Anthology 2015, Brio FAWQ anthology 2015, Elyne Mitchell Writing Awards 2016 and AWAW 2015/2016 and Women's Ink 2018.

Deidre Ryan is a fiction writer based in Melbourne. She works in professional communications.

Jennie Del Mastro is an emerging writer with a passion for playing with reality. She recently won third place in the Lorien Hemingway Short Story Competition. She lives on the south-eastern coast of Australia.

Ashley Kalagian Blunt is a Sydney-based author. Her first book, *My Name Is Revenge*, was shortlisted for the 2019 Woollahra Digital Literary Awards and was a finalist in the 2018 Carmel Bird Digital Literary Award. Her writing appears in *Griffith Review*, *Sydney Review of Books*, *Westerly*, *The Australian*, *The Big Issue* and *Kill Your Darlings*.

Dean MacAllister is a mammal who lives in Melbourne, Australia. He is a seasoned world traveller, scuba diver and avid lover of writing and reading fiction. He has been previously published in multiple magazines, zines and writing competitions worldwide, including *EWR*, *WWC*, *Jitter Press*, *Ricky's Backyard*, is a regular in *Weirdbook* and his first novel, *The Misadventures of a Reluctant Traveller*, is now available on Amazon. For more of his works make sure you check out www.deanmacallister.com

Doug Pender is a former amateur boxer, rugby and cricket player; human resources executive; voracious reader; lover of dance, musicals, movies, sailing and diving in exotic places; husband, writer, father, grandfather. Much of a lot, not a lot of any one thing. Short stories published in *Blue Crow*, *Brio*, *Polestar Writers' Journal*, *NSW Senior Stories*, and *Positive Words*. Novel completed but not yet published.

Rhiannon Raphael doesn't know what she is doing. Sometimes she writes about that and sometimes she writes about lesbian selkies (often the latter.) She has just completed a Master's of Creative Writing, Publishing and Editing at the University of Melbourne and now she works as a publishing assistant. She lives with a cat named Apple Bobbing.

Zena Shapter writes from a castle in a flying city hidden by a thundercloud. Author of *Towards White* (IFWG 2017) and co-author of *Into Tordon* (MidnightSun 2016) among others, she's won over a dozen national writing competitions — including the Australasian Horror Writers' Association Prize, a Ditmar Award, and the Glen Miles Short Story Prize. Her short stories have appeared in *Midnight Echo*, Hugo-nominated *Sci Phi Journal*, *Antipodean SF* and *Award-Winning Australian Writing* (twice). She's a movie buff, traveller, inclusive creativity advocate, and story nerd. She's also a writing mentor, editor, book creator, and short story judge. Find her online at zenashapter.com.

Edwina Shaw is a Brisbane writer of fiction, memoir and screenplays. Since 2002, she has been writing and publishing in Australian and international journals. Her novel, *Thrill Seekers* (Ransom UK) based on her brother's battle with schizophrenia, was shortlisted for the 2012 NSW Premier's Award for New Writing. Her screenplay *M* is currently under development with ScreenQLD. She is also an experienced yoga teacher and runs innovative workshops and retreats combining both writing and yoga.

www.edwinashaw.com
relaxandwriteretreats.blog/
www.speakers-ink.com.au/speakers/edwina-shaw

Matthew R Ward is a Yorkshireman who moved to Australia when he discovered he really enjoys sunlight. He has dabbled with writing for most of his life but only recently started taking it seriously. He likes to write stories that deal with loss, grief, heartbreak and footwear. Matthew has previously had stories published in *Aurealis* and *Andromeda Spaceways*.

At six, almost seven, Keene can't understand what's wrong with Mum. She lies in bed in the spare room, wasting away, even though she's hooked up to a bag that is meant to make her feel better. Dad describes Mum's illness like 'a darkness inside her'. But Keene's sure something else is responsible.

He's sure it's the shadow that's killing her.

One stormy day, Keene decides to go on an adventure into the bush with just his Border Collie, Bunch, in tow – an adventure he's sure will save Mum.

But Keene is not prepared for the dangers he faces.

The Shadow in the Wind is a story of adventure and magical realism as Keene deals with and learns to reconcile events he's too young to fully understand.

Everyone has a book in them. We all have a story we want to share with the world. But where do we start?

The Book Book will help break the process into small, manageable steps, providing invaluable tips, insider knowledge into the publishing industry, as well as the inspiration to get started and to keep writing to the end.

Don't let this opportunity go to waste!

Trust in *The Book Book* to help you find the way.

What exactly is spirit? It is a seemingly abstract and often mind-boggling concept that gets lost in the many other day-to-day things we have to worry about such as caring for our body and, more increasingly, our mental health.

Do you regard your spirit as something akin to your soul, to your outlook and passion in life? Or, do you see it more in the traditional sense of religious practice and prayer?

Healthy Spirit is the third instalment in *The Health Conscious* series, featuring articles from regular people, from a lawyer, to a psychic, to a publisher and almost everything else in between. The articles are written to be insightful, interesting and useful to you in their differing ideas about what spirit is and how to care for it.

You've written and published a book, and you have the first hot copy in your hands.

What next?

Writing and publishing a book is an incredible achievement, and it shouldn't go unheralded. What a book really needs when it comes into the world is a launch to celebrate its arrival. But what does a launch entail?

The Launch Book is a simple guide that will talk you through the requirements of organising a launch and ensure that all your hard work is duly celebrated.

Pinion Press is an imprint of Busybird Publising.

We specialise in publishing a handful of our own titles yearly, trying to combine quality and enjoyability with some altruistic outcome, e.g. raising awareness for a particular condition (as our glorious coffee table photography book, *Walk With Me* – a journal of Kev Howlett's trek up to Mount Everest Base Camp and back – raised awareness of Charcot-Marie-Tooth disease), and/or donate a portion of proceeds for books to various foundations, such as Women Helping Other Women, Breast Cancer Victoria, the Prostate Cancer Foundation, the Epilepsy Foundation, Vision Australia, and the Indigenous Literacy Foundation.

Busybird Publishing is a boutique micropublisher based in the heart of Montmorency, Victoria.

We help authors self-publish. A fee-for-service self-publisher, we make no claims on rights or royalties, and are determined to make sure our authors have a pleasurable, gratifying, and educational journey.

We also run workshops on various forms of writing (fiction, nonfiction, memoir), publishing, and photography, organise writing retreats; host a monthly Open Mic Night (the third Wednesday of every month); and hold competitions to help aspiring writers get published or win mentoring.

To learn more about Busybird Publishing, check out our website at www.busybird.com.au.